The Westie Winter

A STORY OF A
WEST HIGHLAND TERRIER

Look for these books (and more!)
in the Dog Tales series:

One Golden Year

The Westie Winter

Mountain Dog Rescue

DOG TALES #2

The Westie Winter

A STORY OF A
WEST HIGHLAND TERRIER

BY COLEEN HUBBARD

Illustrations by Lori Savastano

AN
APPLE
PAPERBACK

SCHOLASTIC

New York   Toronto   London   Auckland   Sydney

ISBN 0-590-18976-X

12 11 10 9 8 7 6 5 4 3 2 1   8 9/9 0 1 2 3/0

Printed in the U.S.A.   40
First Scholastic printing, November 1998

For Susan and Harvey
and the real-life Oscar

CONTENTS

Brainstorming

"I love Fridays!" said Kelly Brant, between bites of sticky marshmallow.

"Me too," agreed her best friend, Mia Hope-Jones. "Especially the first Friday in December when it's snowing outside and my brothers are gone and you and I can have all the marshmallows we want in our hot chocolate!"

Kelly laughed as Mia plopped another fat marshmallow into her already overflowing cup of steaming cocoa. The two girls were sitting comfortably at Mia's kitchen table, as they did every weekday after school. Kelly and Mia lived three houses away from each other, and Mia's mom, Joni, had been taking care of Kelly after school since both girls were in first grade. Joni always said that the money she earned from baby-sitting was nice, but it was even nicer to have "a part-time second daughter."

Now the girls were in fourth grade together, and they often felt more like sisters than friends — which was fine with Kelly, since she was an only child.

Suddenly, Kelly and Mia heard the sound of a car pulling into the driveway.

"Oh, no!" cried Mia. "It's Perry and Ben! Hide the marshmallows!"

The front door slammed hard, practically shaking the whole house.

Kelly grabbed the bag of marshmallows and slipped it into her lap, sitting up straight and tall in the wooden chair.

Just as she did, Mia's loud and gangly teenage brothers filled the kitchen. Perry was seventeen and drove an ancient red Jeep back and forth to school. Ben, who was fifteen, played guitar in a band and was always going to rehearsals. Both boys were tall and had the same shiny dark hair as Mia.

Perry immediately opened the refrigerator and started drinking milk straight out of the carton.

"Gross!" shouted Mia, giving him a look of disgust. "I'm going to tell Mom!"

"Mom's upstairs in her studio painting those weird fruit Christmas ornaments, and I bet she doesn't want to be bothered," said Perry calmly, taking another big gulp of milk.

"Hey, hot chocolate!" said Ben, lifting Kelly's mug from the table and pretending to take a slurp. "Where are the marshmallows, Kelly-Belly?" The boys always called her Kelly-Belly, and secretly, Kelly didn't really mind. It was the closest she'd ever come to being someone's little sister. But she also knew how tired Mia got of her brothers' constant teasing.

"Get lost, Ben," said Mia. "The marshmallows are gone."

"I don't believe you," Ben responded. He picked up Kelly's two light brown braids and pretended to look underneath them. "Are you hiding them under here?"

Taking the hint, Perry grabbed Mia's black braids and pulled them straight up in the air. "Hey," he said, "what is it with the two of you and your matching braids? Maybe we could braid their heads together, Ben!"

"Leave our hair alone!" shouted Mia. "We'll give you the marshmallows!"

Just in time, Mia's mom walked into the kitchen. Instantly, Ben and Perry dropped the girls' braids and backed away from the table, smiling innocently at their mom. Joni, dressed in paint-splattered denim jeans and a denim shirt with a yellow bandanna in her long black hair, looked suspiciously at the scene before her.

"What's going on?" she asked, eyeing the open refrigerator door and the half-empty milk carton on the table.

"Oh, the usual, Mom," Mia answered. "Ben and Perry are being jerks. They're drinking out of the milk carton and pulling our hair."

"Not true!" Perry protested. "We were admiring their lovely braids. You know how we adore our baby sister and Miss Kelly-Belly."

Just as Joni opened her mouth to speak, Mia's two dogs wandered into the kitchen, adding to the general chaos of the moment. Both dogs were brown and mixed-breed, and getting up there in dog years. They mostly liked to sleep, though they loved a walk around the block with Kelly and Mia.

"Hey, dogs!" cried Kelly, kneeling on the floor to pet Bo and Chubby. "Where have you guys been? Sleeping away the day?"

"No doubt," said Mia. "That's all they do."

Kelly didn't even notice that the bag of marshmallows had fallen out of her lap as she got up. They spilled out of the plastic bag and rolled around the wooden floor, providing tasty and unexpected treats for Bo and Chubby. Both dogs managed to gobble two or three before Mia scooped up the marshmallows.

"I knew you guys were hiding the marshmallows!" said Perry. He spotted one near the dishwasher and ate it right off the floor. "Yum, yum!"

Mia stared at her brother in disbelief. "You have zero manners, Perry."

"That's not true, is it, Mom?" Perry asked Joni. "I am Mr. Manners!"

Joni rolled her eyes at the girls and sent Ben and Perry off to do their homework. She made herself a cup of tea. "You girls okay?" she asked.

"Fine, Mom," said Mia. "Now that the Beast Brothers are gone."

"Then I guess I'll get back to work," Joni sighed. "I have about a hundred more glass ornaments to paint before the university art sale next week."

"Are you still saving me one?" asked Kelly. "I want to buy one to give my mom for Christmas. She loves those ones with pears and apples painted on them."

"I'll save you my best one," Joni promised. "And for you, a special deal on the price. I know how much you and Mia make in allowance."

"But at least she doesn't have two hulking brothers to buy gifts for!" Mia complained. "I should just get them each five gallons of milk and twenty pounds of cookies."

"I *do* have an extra gift to buy this year," Kelly remembered. "Grandpa Duncan."

"That's right," said Joni. "This will be his first Christmas living with your family."

"He's so cool," added Mia. "You're lucky. My grandparents live really far away."

"He *is* cool," Kelly agreed.

"How come his last name isn't Brant, like yours?" Mia asked.

"He's my mom's dad," Kelly explained. "Her maiden name was McBride, too."

"It's so great you all get to be together," said Joni.

"But I have no idea what to get him for Christmas. Help me think of something." Kelly looked from Mia to Joni, hoping they had a great idea.

"I'd better get back to work," said Joni. "I'll leave you girls to brainstorm."

Kelly, still sitting on the kitchen floor near the dogs, leaned down to plant kisses on Bo's and

Chubby's silky heads. "I know what I want for Christmas," she sighed. "Same as every year. A dog. And same as every year, I won't get one. I think *you're* the lucky one, to have two dogs."

"Maybe your parents will let you have one this year." Mia adjusted her fashionable glasses, which had small, stop-sign-shaped wire frames. "You're old enough to take care of a dog, which is their usual argument against getting one."

"It's not that so much," Kelly explained. "It's because Mom and Dad work all day, and I'm at school, and they think it would be unfair to leave a dog all alone with no company."

"They're right about that. Dogs do like to have people around. Bo and Chubby hang out all day with my mom up in her studio."

"That must be nice for her, too," said Kelly. "If I worked at home, I'd want to have a dog to hang out with."

"She likes it," said Mia. "But no one pets our dogs as much as you do. When you're around, they're in heaven."

"That's because I love your cute furry faces," Kelly said to the dogs. "I love your cute noses, and your sweet eyes, and the way you smell, and —"

"And your bad breath and your hair that sticks all over our clothes," Mia continued. "Don't forget that part!"

"I don't think you have bad breath," Kelly said, stroking Chubby's nose. "You just have dog breath." Chubby let out a contented sigh, delighted by all the attention he was getting. Bo waited patiently for his turn.

"Let's go play on the computer," Mia suggested. "My dad installed a new game that lets you design houses and buildings." Mia's dad, David, was a computer genius who installed new computer systems in schools, so Mia always had the latest games and programs.

"Okay. But first, help me think of what to get Grandpa Dunc for Christmas."

"Let's see," said Mia, closing her eyes and tilting her head back. "Let me think about this." Mia liked to say that she was visual like her mother and that if she could picture something, she could arrive at an answer.

"He finally got all his furniture and things shipped from California," Kelly said. "It's all set up in the carriage house."

"I love the carriage house," said Mia. They were talking about the separate house on Kelly's property, which had been a storage room for horse-drawn carriages a hundred years ago. "It's so cute — like a gingerbread house!"

"Grandpa likes it because he still has his privacy, but he can be with us whenever he wants. He even has his own address because the carriage house faces the street behind us."

"Do you think he's lonely without your grandma?" Mia asked sympathetically. "If I were married to someone for fifty years and then he died, I'd be pretty lonely."

"I think he's lonely some of the time," Kelly explained. "But my grandma died four years ago, so he's had a while to get used to it. It took him ages to agree with my mom that he should come to Redville to live."

"Why?" asked Mia. "You're his only grandkid, and your mom is his only kid."

"I know. I come from a long line of only children. Weird, huh?"

"I think only kids have a lot of benefits — like getting more attention, for one thing. And no nasty brothers to tease you all day long."

"Maybe." Kelly shrugged. "Ben and Perry aren't so bad. Sometimes they're pretty nice. Like the time they helped us build the tree house in my backyard."

"True," Mia admitted. "But you don't have to live with them."

"Talking about me?" asked Perry, appearing in the kitchen. "Talking about what a great guy I am, how I look after my little sister and my extra little sister? How I drive you places in my awesome Jeep?" Perry rummaged through the cupboard until he found a fresh bag of pretzels.

"We were talking about my grandpa and what to get him for Christmas," Kelly said, still petting the sleeping dogs.

"Hey, Duncan's a great guy!" said Perry. "He showed me his collection of antique tools. Told me all about the antique store he had in California."

"That's the love of his life — antiques!" said Kelly. "He says that besides being with us, the best thing about the Midwest is all the antiques. Every weekend we drive around looking for old saws and hammers and stuff."

"Then get him a hammer or saw," said Perry, crunching pretzels.

"He likes to pick them out himself. Hunting for them is the fun part, I guess."

"How about a tie?" said Perry.

"He never wears ties. He's from California, re-member?"

"Right." Perry laughed. "How about a book?"

"He has hundreds."

"True." Perry drummed his hands on the coun-tertop, playing to an imaginary tune. "The dude is one big reader. He showed me his book collection, too. I give up, Kelly-Belly. I'm at a loss."

"Hey," said Mia slowly. She opened her eyes and stood up from her chair. "I saw it! I saw it in my mind! The perfect gift!"

"What?" asked Kelly. "What is it?"

"Well, I pictured him in the carriage house, surrounded by books and antiques, happy to be with your family, but . . . sad sometimes. Lonely."

"How can I help with that?" asked Kelly. "Mom and Dad want him to try some of the classes they offer for seniors at the university, but he doesn't seem very interested."

"He needs company when you and your mom and dad are gone during the day."

"Who? What? How can I do that, Mia?"

"The answer is right before your eyes, silly," Mia said with a laugh.

Kelly looked in front of her. All she could see were Perry's legs, covered in baggy jeans, ending in sneakers that were tapping out a rhythm on the wood floor. "Perry? Perry is my answer?"

"I am?" said Perry, stopping his drumming for a moment. "Cool."

"Not Perry! Look down," urged Mia.

Kelly looked down at Chubby and Bo snoozing contentedly. "Bo and Chubby are the answer? I'm very confused."

"Dogs!" shouted Mia. "Or at least one dog."

"You think I should get Grandpa Dunc a dog?" Kelly asked, her eyes wide with surprise.

"Think about it," urged Mia. "It's perfect." Her brown eyes shone with excitement. "You get him a dog for Christmas. Then he has company and you get your wish of having a dog! It's perfect!"

Kelly was silent, considering Mia's idea. It *was* perfect! But how would she ever convince her parents to agree? And how would she go about finding the right dog and getting it home and — it was too overwhelming.

Finally, Kelly stood up and brushed dog hair from her hands. "My parents would never let me," she concluded.

"Here's what you do," said Perry, spreading his

hands out wide and shrugging. "It's easy. You have
to appeal to their humanity. Remember, Kelly-
Belly, your parents are ex-hippies turned college
professors. They support all these humane causes
from growing up in the nineteen sixties. They are
majorly great people. Very hip, very involved. So,
explain to them that it would be *humane* for your
grandpa to have a companion in his twilight years.
Everyone knows the benefits that pets can bring to
people who live alone."

"He's not alone," Kelly interrupted. "He has
us."

"Sure," said Perry. "But you know what I
mean. He spends his days alone, until you guys all
get home. A dog would be a boost to his physical
and emotional health. They did a whole program
about it on public television."

"Perry, you're a genius!" shouted Mia, running
over to give her brother a hug. "Sometimes you
are brilliant and even sort of nice."

"Can I get you to put that on videotape so I can

play it for Mom?" Perry teased. "It would be my Christmas present to her."

"Do you really think it would work?" asked Kelly. "Because I think it's brilliant, too. I think giving Grandpa a dog is the perfect thing. Sometimes I sit at school and think about him being alone and it makes me sad."

"All you can do is try," said Perry. "Tell your parents that your only other idea is a tie."

The doorbell rang, and Bo and Chubby scrambled to their feet, barking.

"What time is it?" asked Kelly.

"Five," said Perry, looking at his watch.

"That's your mom, then," said Mia, heading for the door. "Are you going to ask her?"

"I'd better wait until later. She doesn't like me to ask for things in front of other people. She likes to have time to think."

"That's because she's a math professor," Perry explained. "Mathematicians like to ponder and analyze."

"Hi, honey! Hi, Perry," said Kelly's mom, following Mia into the kitchen.

"Hey, Laura," said Perry. "How is the Institution of Higher Learning?"

"Fine." Laura took off her winter hat and shook her short brown curls. "But I'm glad it's Friday. What have you guys been up to?"

"Not much," said Perry, winking at Kelly. "I've just been explaining how the world works to these fine young ladies."

"Great!" said Laura. "Maybe you can explain it to me next."

"No problem," said Perry. "Always glad to help."

Mia punched him on the arm as he left the kitchen with an almost empty bag of pretzels.

"Is your mom painting?" asked Laura.

"Christmas ornaments!" Mia replied, pointing upstairs.

"Right," said Laura, nodding. "Well, I won't interrupt her. Ready to go home, Kelly? I thought we'd order pizza for dinner. I'm too tired to cook."

"Great," said Kelly, giving her mom a hug. Then she looked at Mia and winked. "You won't believe it, but Mia and I came up with absolutely the most perfect Christmas present in the whole world to give to Grandpa Dunc!"

TWO

Kelly Presents Her Plan

"Mom, I have something important to talk to you about," said Kelly.

She and Laura stood side by side at the kitchen sink, washing lettuce for a salad. Laura had changed from her work clothes into comfortable leggings and a blue woolly sweater. The pizza was on its way, and Kelly's dad would soon be home from his last class at the university.

"Can you wait just a second?" asked Laura. "I want to put some Christmas music on the stereo. I need some help getting into the holiday spirit."

"Why?" asked Kelly, though she had a feeling she already knew. Each December, Kelly's parents became frantically busy giving final exams to their classes, grading papers, and advising students for the coming semester. It would be several weeks until the "end of term craziness" was over and her parents could concentrate on the holidays.

"Too many math exams!" said Laura, waving her hand in front of her face as she headed for the living room.

"I knew it," Kelly said. "And too many history exams for Dad. Every year it's the same thing!"

Kelly hoped her parents would be able to focus on her idea of getting a dog for Grandpa Dunc. She needed them to understand and agree to the plan. And she didn't have much time before Christmas to put everything in place.

But before Laura could return to the kitchen, the pizza delivery woman rang the doorbell. And shortly after that, Kelly's dad walked in the front door, and Grandpa Dunc walked in the back door. There was no time to talk now.

"Hey, kiddo!" said Duncan, gathering Kelly in his arms for a big hug. "How's my favorite grandkid?"

Duncan was a tall and elegant man of seventy-five, with thick white hair and tan glasses. He had on a green parka and a furry hat, which he had worn constantly since moving from California to a much colder climate.

"I'm your *only* grandkid!" Kelly answered. "Remember?"

"That's why you're my favorite! How was school and what's for dinner?"

"Fine and pizza."

"Pizza!" said Duncan. "I like the pizza in this town. Regular pizza — not the funny kinds they have in California with fruit and nuts and herbs on them."

"Redville is a college town," said Laura, coming into the kitchen. "You have to have good pizza in a town filled with thousands of hungry students."

"Hey, everyone!" said Kelly's dad as he, too, appeared in the crowded kitchen. "How's it going?"

Kelly hugged her dad, happy to see him. He was shorter than Grandpa Dunc and had much less hair. It was a family joke that Duncan had a full head of hair at seventy-five while John had very little left at forty-five.

Dinner was lively that night, with everyone sharing parts of their day and trying to recall moments that would amuse the others. Laura told about almost slipping on the ice outside a classroom and spilling a cup of coffee onto the snow. "It made a coffee snow cone," she explained, "and I was tempted to eat it."

"I found an antique branding iron at a little shop outside of town," offered Duncan. "Used for cattle, probably fifty years ago. A good find! And I'm enjoying driving around the back roads of Redville."

Duncan had brought his old red pickup truck with him from California, and Kelly's dad said Duncan was one of the best drivers he'd ever seen. Kelly was just glad her grandpa had a way to get to the places he needed to go to.

"I started my Christmas shopping," John said mysteriously, looking at Kelly. "At the campus bookstore."

"Not another University of Redville sweatshirt," joked Kelly. "I have about ten of those."

"Nope, not a sweatshirt," John answered. "And that's all I'm saying."

"Speaking of Christmas," put in Duncan, wiping a dab of pizza sauce off his chin, "I haven't heard what you might be wishing for, Kelly."

"I don't know. I haven't thought about it too much. Have you thought about what you want, Grandpa?"

"I don't need a thing," he answered predictably. Grown-ups always said things like that. "Being here with all of you is the best gift I could have."

"No, it's a gift for *us*," said Laura, her voice breaking a little. "We couldn't be happier that you moved here."

Kelly was beginning to see how much it meant to her mom to have Grandpa Dunc nearby. And she noticed that whenever Laura talked about it, she always got a little teary.

Duncan patted Laura's hand and smiled. Then he turned his attention back to Kelly. "I want to get you something really special, kiddo. So you start thinking about what that could be."

Kelly promised, but she knew it wouldn't be easy. Thoughts of dogs filled her head, leaving little room for anything else. She could hardly wait for a moment alone with her parents. She was practically bursting with the need to share her plan.

"What is your class doing for the school holiday show this year, honey?" John asked Kelly. "What's the theme?"

"It's about how all the different winter holidays are celebrated around the world," Kelly explained. "Our class is doing Chinese New Year. We just started our research today."

"That sounds terrific," said Duncan. "May I come?"

"Of course, silly! It's a family event. Right, Mom?"

"Right. Every year. Followed by ice-cream sundaes at the Dairy Barn."

"Then I'm definitely coming! Now, how about if I do the dishes, since you guys did the cooking?"

"You mean the ordering," joked Laura. "I just

picked up the phone and — instant dinner!"

Kelly leaped at the opportunity to leave Duncan in the kitchen. She could lure her parents up to her room with a pretend question about homework, even though she never did schoolwork on Friday nights.

"Have a seat," Kelly told her parents, clearing off her desk chair and a spot at the end of her bed. "We need to talk."

Kelly was not famous for having a neat room, though she did try. She always made her bed and put her clothes away, but every available surface was stacked with books and papers, art supplies, and small collections of rocks, horse figurines, and antique music boxes that Duncan had sent to her over the years from his shop in California.

"Sounds serious," said John. "What's up?"

"This isn't about homework, is it?" Laura guessed.

Kelly cleared her throat, took a deep breath, and began. "I want to get Grandpa a dog for

Christmas — and don't interrupt just yet! Mia and I were talking about how Grandpa might sometimes be lonely when we've gone to work and school. And Perry said that dogs make excellent companions for older people and even help them be more healthy. He saw it on public television."

"Honey, what makes you think Grandpa is lonely?" Laura asked. "Has he said something to you?"

"No," Kelly admitted. "He seems pretty happy, but a dog would be good company for him and —"

"Kelly, getting a dog is a serious matter. It's a huge responsibility. It's a lot different from giving someone a sweater or a pair of slippers," said John.

"But it's better than slippers, don't you see? It's something living! And didn't he and Grandma always have dogs in California?"

"Yes," said Laura. "They always had dogs. I grew up with animals. But we had several acres of land, Kelly. The dogs had room to run and play."

"That's true," agreed John. "But it's also true that Duncan loves animals."

"Right!" Kelly insisted. "Don't you see? It's perfect! And we have a fenced yard."

"A pretty small one," Laura reminded.

"Then I could get him a small dog," Kelly countered.

"I don't know," said John, scratching his head. "It's a sweet idea, honey, but it's pretty risky."

"Why?"

"Because," said Laura, taking over, "what if Grandpa didn't like the dog? What if the dog wasn't healthy, or turned out to be mean, or couldn't adjust?"

"You're only thinking of the negative things," Kelly replied. "What if it turned out to be really great? What if we found a wonderful dog and Grandpa loved it, and it kept him company, and reminded him of happy times when he and Grandma had dogs in California? You always tell me to look on the positive side of a situation, so why can't you?"

John and Laura were silent for a few moments, regarding Kelly with admiration. She had made some convincing arguments, and they were people who liked a lively debate — whether with their students or their daughter.

"Have you given some thought to how you would go about locating the perfect dog?" asked John. "If we decide to go forward with this plan?"

"I have, Dad. And I think you'll approve, because it involves research. We all know how much you love research!"

Laura laughed and reached over to put an arm around John. "She knows us so well it's scary!"

"Mia and I are going to find some books on dogs and read about all the different breeds. Can you take us to the university library tomorrow, Dad?"

"Tomorrow?" asked John. "Hold on a minute. We haven't agreed to this yet."

"What more can I say?" Kelly asked, shrugging her shoulders. "It's a perfect plan."

"Well," said Laura, "first of all, there's the question of money. If you go to a breeder, it will cost a fair amount of money. Even if you go to an animal shelter, there are adoption fees, medical exams and shots, tags, collars, food, leashes, training — it's a big investment."

"I've thought of that, and I have a few ideas," said Kelly.

"Then there's the matter of time," put in John. "The time involved in training, housebreaking, all of that. How can we be sure that Grandpa wants to give that kind of time to an animal?"

"And the biggest concern of all," continued Laura, "is that sometimes surprises can backfire."

"What do you mean?" Kelly asked. "Surprises are great!"

"They are," Laura agreed, "but sometimes the person being surprised doesn't react the way you want them to. Sometimes they're too overwhelmed by the surprise, or it makes them feel a little strange or powerless. You're probably too young to remember, honey, but one year Dad decided to throw me a surprise birthday party —"

"Oh, boy!" groaned John, holding his head. "Was that ever a disaster!"

"What happened?" Kelly didn't remember this story.

"Well, Dad planned the whole thing very carefully. He had all our friends come over to the house at a certain time. He had balloons and decorations everywhere, and food and gifts. It was such a lovely idea!"

"But," said John, "I forgot that Mom was coming home right from swimming at the university pool."

"Right." Laura laughed. "There I was in my sweatpants, with my hair dripping wet and no makeup on, and all my friends, dressed in their nicest party clothes, were yelling, 'Surprise!' "

"Oh, no!" Kelly moaned sympathetically. "Poor Mom! What did you do?"

"Well, after I got over the shock and stopped

being mad at your father, I went upstairs and changed and dried my hair."

"And then she enjoyed the party. Right?" John asked hopefully.

"Yes, then it was a wonderful party. But the point of the story is that surprises can be messy. They don't always go exactly as planned."

"I see your point," Kelly admitted. "But can you picture Grandpa having this great dog for a companion while we're gone? Perry says dogs can even help people live longer lives! And we all want Grandpa to live a long, long time!"

"Yes, we do," Laura said quietly. "We want Grandpa to have a long and happy life."

"So?" Kelly asked. "What do you think? Can I do it?"

"Hey," John said. "Slow down. What about the money part? You'd better discuss that part of the equation with Math Mom and see if it all adds up!" John laughed heartily at his own joke, while Kelly and Laura rolled their eyes at his silly puns.

"Yes," said Laura, playing along, "I hate to sub-tract from your excitement, but an animal can re-ally multiply household expenses."

"I have a hundred dollars in my savings ac-count," Kelly said firmly. "And I could do extra chores around the house for the next few weeks to —"

"Like cleaning your room?" John suggested.

"Kelly, you've been saving that money for two years. It's supposed to be for a new bike, or some-thing significant," said Laura.

"This *is* something significant!" cried Kelly. "Please say yes!"

"You would really spend your entire savings on Grandpa's gift?" John asked. "That's very gener-ous, honey."

"Of course," said Laura, "it's sort of a two-way gift, isn't it? Grandpa gets a dog, and by extension you finally get your wish of having a dog, too."

"Well," Kelly said, trying not to smile, "I would have to be around the dog, too. As a member of the family. Please? Please can I do it?"

"You know what?" said Laura. "I think you should give Dad and me a chance to talk it over. This is a complicated undertaking, and I'd like some time to analyze the situation."

"Because you're a math teacher, right?" said Kelly.

"Mostly because I'm a parent." Laura laughed. "Can we give you an answer in the morning?"

Kelly sighed. She was hoping for an answer immediately but she knew she had to be patient. "Okay, in the morning. In the *early* morning."

"We'd better get back downstairs before Duncan thinks something is going on," said John. "We'll talk about it in the morning."

Kelly's parents left her sitting on her bed, knowing she wouldn't sleep a wink that night. She'd be up counting dogs instead of sheep.

Please, she thought, *please say yes! Please tell me I can get a dog for Grandpa Dunc. It will be the best Christmas ever!*

THREE

The Research Begins

On Saturday morning, Kelly was awake before it was even light outside. She pulled on her robe, shivering, and tried to find her slippers in the jumbled mess of her closet. Giving up, she hurried down the hall to her parents' bedroom and stood at the foot of their bed.

They looked so peaceful she hated to wake them. But she had to have an answer. She had to know what they had decided about the dog! She cleared her throat and waited for any sign of movement. Her father stirred a bit and turned over. Kelly tapped her mother's foot beneath the quilt and waited some more, but nothing happened. They were deep in sleep. They looked as if they could sleep until noon!

Desperate, Kelly threw herself forward, falling with a thud between her parents. That did it! They both started, trying to figure out what foreign object had just made an unexpected landing in the middle of their bed.

"K-Kelly!" stuttered Laura. "Is that you?"

"Is everything okay?" asked John, his voice groggy and hoarse.

"Fine." Kelly smiled. "Have a good sleep?"

"We *were* having a good sleep," Laura said, sitting up. "What are you doing up so early? It's weeks until Christmas. Are you sick?"

"No, but speaking of Christmas," Kelly began, "did you guys decide about the dog? You said you'd have an answer in the morning."

"By that," said John, sitting up as well, "I think we meant the part of the morning when it's light outside and we've had our breakfast."

"Sorry. I couldn't help it. I hardly slept all night thinking about dogs."

Laura laughed, pushing her hands through her tangled curls. "When you get an idea in your head, you really hold on to it, don't you?"

"Just like your mother." John sighed and flopped down, pulling a pillow over his head.

"I can't stand the suspense!" cried Kelly. "Tell me before I burst."

"*Goaheadandgetthedog*," came John's muffled reply from underneath the pillow.

"What? What did you say?"

"He said," translated Laura, "to go ahead and get the dog. We talked about it, and we decided you could go ahead with this project — on one condition."

"What?" said Kelly, bursting with joy. "Anything! Name your terms!"

John uncovered his head and sat up. "You have to take responsibility for finding the right dog. And if the surprise backfires and Grandpa doesn't want the dog, then you become the sole caretaker of the animal. Agreed?"

"Agreed!" shouted Kelly. "Thank you, thank you, thank you! You won't regret this, I promise."

"I already regret it," moaned John, putting two pillows over his head.

"Just to show you how grateful I am, I'm going to go downstairs and make breakfast. You guys just relax and get some more beauty sleep. I'll take care of everything!"

In the kitchen, Kelly found Grandpa Dunc sitting at the table, drinking coffee and looking at the telephone book. When he heard Kelly come in, he snapped the book shut and nudged it aside. He folded a piece of paper and tucked it into his shirt pocket.

"Hey, Grandpa. You're up early, too."

"Couldn't sleep. Too much to do today."

"Hey, me too!" Kelly grinned, loving the feeling of carrying her surprise safe inside her. Her grandfather didn't have a clue what she was up to!

"What's with the phone book?" she asked, sitting down at the table.

"Oh, nothing," answered Duncan. "I realized I don't have one in the carriage house, so I came over to borrow yours. I needed to look up the number of a friend."

Kelly hadn't realized that Duncan had made friends in Redville already. But he was certainly a friendly man, so it didn't surprise her too much.

"What's his name?" asked Kelly. "Your new friend."

"Who said it was a *him*?"

"It's a *her*?" Now this was surprising.

"Gotcha!" teased Duncan. "Made your jaw drop, didn't I?"

Kelly gulped and tried to look normal. "No, I just —"

Duncan laughed at Kelly's stammering. "Actually, honey, I was just looking up some more antique places."

"Is that what you're going to do today? Hunt for more antiques?"

"I'm definitely going to do some hunting!" Duncan smiled, taking Kelly's hand. "What about you? What are you plans for this fine snowy Saturday?"

"I don't know." Kelly yawned, trying to sound casual. "I may go to the library to do some research."

"School project?"

"Big project." Kelly nodded. "Got to get started. I need to have it all finished before Christmas."

Just then the phone rang, making both Kelly and Duncan jump.

"Hello?" said Kelly, wondering who would call so early. It was Mia, asking how things had gone with the dog idea. Kelly was excited to share the good news, but she realized she couldn't talk with her grandpa right there.

Instead, she spoke in careful code, hoping her friend would understand. "Mia," she said, "I was wondering if you wanted to go to the library with me today, to do some research on our — on, you know, our *project*. The one that has to be finished by *Christmas*? I was just telling my *grandfather* about it. I think my dad could drive us after lunch."

After a few seconds, Mia caught on. "Did they say yes?" she asked. "Just say yes or no."

"Yes," said Kelly, trying to sound neutral. "So, the library?"

On the other end of the line, Mia screamed with delight at the news and agreed to come over to Kelly's house right after lunch.

As Kelly hung up, she smiled at Grandpa Dunc, realizing for the first time how hard it might be to keep her secret all the way until Christmas.

After lunch, John drove Kelly and Mia to the university library. He had some papers to grade, so he didn't mind the trip at all. He helped the girls get settled at a long wooden table and showed them where they would find books about dogs.

"I'll be over there, by the window," he told them. "Come get me if you need anything, or ask the research librarian. And no goofing around — everyone here is studying for finals."

"We know that, Dad," said Kelly. "We'll be quiet."

Surveying the shelves, both girls were surprised at how many books about dogs there were. "Look," said Kelly. "There are books on dog breeds, dog care, dog training, dog grooming —"

"And look here," added Mia. "There are even books on the emotional life of dogs and what to do when your dog is depressed!"

"Wow. I didn't know dogs could be depressed."

"Sure," said Mia. "You've seen Bo and Chubby when no one is paying them any attention. They look all sad, and their tails droop, and they just lie around."

"Well, for now," Kelly decided, "I think we should look at the books on dog breeds. Later we can read about dog emotions."

The girls each carried a huge stack of books over to the table, trying to be very quiet as they sorted them out. Kelly chose a thick hardcover book with colored pictures of different kinds of dogs on every page. Mia scooted closer, and together they turned the glossy pages. There were small dogs, big dogs, hairy and nearly hairless dogs. There were dogs with curly tails, shaggy tails, and droopy tails. Long ears, stand-up ears, and fluffy ears. Brown coats, white coats, tan coats, black coats, red coats, gold coats, and every combination of colors.

"I had no idea there were this many kinds of dogs in the world!" whispered Kelly.

"I know!" agreed Mia. "It's kind of overwhelming."

"Look at this one," said Kelly, pointing to a picture of a large red-brown dog with a thick coat, foxlike head, and curly tail. "It's called a Finnish spitz."

"It sounds like you're saying, 'Finish spitting!' "

Kelly laughed at Mia's joke, covering her mouth with her hand so as not to make noise. "But

it's a beautiful dog, isn't it? It says they were originally raised to hunt bears."

"Cool!" said Mia. "But I don't think your grandpa is going to be hunting bears."

"No. The only thing he hunts for is antiques."

"Oh, look at this one. A Hanoverian Schweisshund."

"A what?" asked Kelly.

"It's supposed to be brave and intelligent, with a keen scenting ability."

"Nice," said Kelly. "But I don't think I should get a dog whose name I can't pronounce."

"True," agreed Mia. "Hey, look at this one!"

Kelly grabbed the page. "Is that a dog or a lamb?" The animal had a pear-shaped head and short, curly white hair.

"It's a dog," said Mia, reading. "But it looks just like a lamb. It's called a Bedlington terrier. It's a British breed, originally used to chase rats out of mine tunnels."

"Yuck! That wouldn't be a fun job."

"Maybe to a dog." Mia shrugged.

"This one's neat looking," said Kelly. "Rhodesian Ridgeback. From South Africa. Once used to hunt lions!"

"Oh, I've seen one of those before," said Mia. "They're huge, and they have this ridge of hair on their back that stands up. It says they're good family dogs."

"But it's so big!" said Kelly. "I don't think we can have a dog that big with our small yard."

"Let's look at little dogs, then," said Mia, flipping to another chapter of the huge book. There they found spaniels and terriers and funny little dogs with long hair covering their eyes and hard-to-pronounce names.

After that they looked at pictures of familiar dogs — Dalmatians, collies, German shepherds, sheepdogs, retrievers, and poodles.

"I'm lost," said Kelly finally, putting her head down on the table. "So many kinds of dogs! I'll never be able to pick just one!"

"I know," agreed Mia, giving in to a big yawn. "I'm glad I didn't have to pick my dogs — they just found us."

"That would be perfect," said Kelly. "If this incredible stray dog without a home just wandered into my life. Some dog like Bo or Chubby! But what are the chances of that happening in time for Christmas?"

"Not likely," said Mia. "What are you going to do?"

Before Kelly could think of an answer, her dad appeared at their table. He ruffled Kelly's hair and asked how things were going.

"Terrible!" moaned Kelly. "Look how many kinds of dogs there are! My head is spinning."

John looked at the spread of books on the table. "These are all about specific breeds?"

"Yep," said Mia. "And believe me, there are some strange ones!"

"Well, I have an idea," he said. "Instead of looking only at breed, you could look at personality."

"How?" asked Kelly.

"By doing some hands-on research at an animal shelter," John explained. "That way you could meet and observe some actual animals, instead of just looking at pictures and reading about breed characteristics."

"Yes!" said Mia. "We could meet some nice mixed-breed dogs like Bo and Chubby!"

"Picking an animal just by how it looks seems a little like shopping for a certain color sweater. There should be something about the dog that appeals to you on a personal level," John said. "That way, this whole experience will be more meaningful for both you and Grandpa."

"Good point," said Mia.

"He always makes good points." Kelly smiled. "That's why he's a professor!"

"Tell you what," John continued. "I'll take you girls over to the shelter tomorrow. How would that be?"

"Great, Dad!" said Kelly. "We really appreciate your help."

"Okay." John grinned. "Just don't ask for my

help when it's time to use the 'pooper scooper' in our backyard this summer. I mean it! That's your job!"

Kelly and Mia laughed until a tall and somber librarian held his finger to his lips and pointed to all the quiet, busy students.

Still shaking with giggles, Mia and Kelly returned their enormous pile of books, finished with the first phase of their research.

FOUR

The Animal Shelter

On Sunday morning, Kelly had another brilliant idea.

"Mom," she began, "tell me what you think about this. When Dad takes Mia and me to the animal shelter today, I'll invite Grandpa to come along!"

"But I thought the whole thing was supposed to be a surprise. Won't he catch on if he goes with you?"

"I've got it all figured out," Kelly explained. "He won't have to know we're looking at dogs to adopt. He'll just think that we're going to look around, the way we sometimes do."

"But why bring him along, Kelly?" asked Laura. She was sipping her coffee and trying to grade tests at the dining room table. Sheets of paper with complicated math equations stood in stacks before her. "Am I missing something? Is my brain fried from all these numbers?"

Kelly laughed, realizing she'd left out the most important part of her idea. "Mom, if Grandpa comes, I can observe him looking at dogs. I can see what kinds of dogs he likes. I'll just sort of follow behind and watch."

"Are you training for a career as a spy?"

"Maybe," Kelly joked. "Anything besides grading math papers!"

Laura stretched and put her pen down. "Math can be fun, you know," she said. "Someday you'll believe me."

"You don't look as if you're having much fun," Kelly pointed out. "Why don't you take a break and come with us to the animal shelter?"

Just then, Duncan walked in the kitchen door. Kelly could hear him whistling Christmas carols as he made his way toward the dining room.

"Good morning!" he boomed in his deep voice.

"How are my favorite granddaughter and my favorite math professor?"

"I'm great!" answered Kelly. "The math professor isn't so great. She has bags under her eyes and cramps in her fingers."

"You need to take a break, Laura," said Duncan. "It's actually a beautiful day outside. Cold, but with lots of sunshine!"

Kelly knew her grandpa still hadn't adjusted to how gray the Midwest winters were. Sometimes the sun didn't shine for days at a time — unlike the California town Duncan had left behind. Kelly was always glad when the sun came out, because she knew it made her grandpa happy.

"I was just telling Mom to take a break," explained Kelly. "I want her to come with us to the animal shelter. And can you come, too, Grandpa?"

Duncan looked surprised by the offer. He studied his granddaughter carefully. "You want me to come to the animal shelter?" he repeated.

"Yes," Kelly said. "Please do. Dad's taking Mia and me, just to look around. We like to look at all the dogs — and cats, too. And sometimes there are rabbits and birds."

"Are you still pestering your mom and dad for a dog? Seems to me that's what you've asked Santa for every year since you were old enough to talk!"

"True," Kelly admitted. "I can't help it. I just love dogs!"

"But we're never home," put in Laura, trying to help save Kelly's surprise. "It wouldn't be fair to the dog."

"Maybe so," Duncan said, considering. "But it might be good company when you *are* around."

"Do you miss having dogs?" Kelly switched into spy mode. Any information she could pry out of Duncan would help her cause.

"Sure," Duncan admitted. "I always liked having dogs around. But then, we lived out in the country. Plenty of room for them to run around."

"What was your absolute favorite dog ever?" Kelly tried to sound very, very casual — as if she were just making conversation.

Duncan was silent, rubbing his large hand across his chin. Kelly noticed that he was freshly shaved and was wearing one of his nicest sweaters. Where was he going? Did he already have plans?

"I don't recall that I ever had a favorite dog, Kelly," he finally answered. "I loved each of them, and they were all very different. Hey, Laura — remember that funny-looking old yellow dog we had when you were about ten?"

Laura smiled, remembering. "You mean Big Pete? How could I forget! He was this huge, slobbering yellow Lab who wanted to lick every single person who ever came inside our house. You know how some dogs like to bark at the mail carrier? Well, Big Pete liked to lick him!"

"And the worst part about it was that Big Pete had really terrible breath!" added Duncan. "Whew!"

Laura and Duncan laughed at the memory, and Kelly made a mental note to be on the lookout for yellow dogs. But not huge ones with bad breath.

"So, will you come with us?" asked Kelly. "Just for fun?"

"Sure," said Duncan, "that might be just what I need to do today. How about you, Laura?"

"I can't," she moaned. "If I don't stick with this, I'll never finish grading these, and I have to return them to my students tomorrow."

"Spoilsport," kidded Duncan.

"Math Mom!" added Kelly.

At the Redville Animal Shelter, the parking lot was nearly full. John drove around and around, looking for a spot.

"Why is it so crowded?" asked Kelly, sitting forward anxiously.

"The holidays are a busy time for animal shelters," John answered. "Lots of people want a cute little puppy to put under the tree."

"Really?" Kelly tried to keep the excitement out of her voice. "Lucky them!" She nudged Mia, who nudged her back. "But we're just here to look around, right, Mia?"

"Right!" Mia said. "It's fun to just hang out here and see all the dogs — and cats!"

But inside the long, low building, the girls quickly discovered another reason why the shelter was so busy. A special holiday fund-raiser was in progress. A very authentic-looking Santa sat in an oversized chair, posing for pictures with groups of people and their pets.

"You mean to tell me," said Duncan, "that these folks all brought in their pets, just to have pictures taken with Santa?"

"I guess so," said John, studying a sign on the wall. "It says here that it costs ten dollars, and that the proceeds go toward keeping the shelter operating. It's kind of silly, but it's for a good cause."

"It's not silly!" protested Kelly. "I think it's cool!"

"Yeah," said Mia. "It's really cute. I wish I'd brought Bo and Chubby!"

All around them, dogs barked and cats cried out. The smell of animals and disinfectant was thick in the air. Volunteers directed traffic, took money for photos, answered questions, and handed out informational flyers about the shelter.

"I bet this place is as busy today as any shopping mall," said John, looking around. "Which direction shall we go, girls?"

"How about if we just walk around and look," Kelly suggested.

"The kennels are over there to the right," said Mia.

"Let's go, then," said Duncan, heading off. "Let's go say hello to some of these poor critters."

Kelly and Mia purposefully fell behind Duncan and John so that they could carry out their spy mission. Kelly took a tiny notebook and pencil from her coat pocket, ready to record any necessary information. But John and Duncan spent only a few moments in front of each glassed-in kennel, watching the animal for a bit, reading the sign that gave basic information, and then moving on.

"He doesn't seem very interested yet," noted

Mia. "He hasn't stopped anywhere for very long."

"True," agreed Kelly. "Maybe it's because my dad is with him. I think we need to separate them."

"Good idea. Call him over."

"Hey, Dad!" called Kelly. "Could you come here for a minute?"

John looked back at the girls and then excused himself from Duncan. "What is it?" He looked from Kelly to Mia. "What are you two plotting now?"

"We need you to stay away from Grandpa," Kelly explained.

"Why?" asked John, not understanding.

"Because he's just talking to you and not stopping to bond with any of the dogs. If you leave him alone, he may find one he likes," Kelly elaborated.

"Oh, okay," said John. "I get it. I was being a distraction."

"Exactly," said Mia. "No offense!"

"None taken. I think I'll just go over that way

and look at the cats. Not that I particularly like cats. How about if I meet you by Santa Claus in about twenty minutes?"

"Perfect," said Kelly. "Thanks, Dad."

After John left, Kelly and Mia tiptoed toward Duncan. They spotted him watching a Dalmatian puppy.

"Dalmatian," Kelly wrote on her blank notebook page.

"It's cute," said Mia. "But my mom told me that Dalmatians can't take the cold because their coats are thin. They have to be inside in the winter."

"That wouldn't be good if you live in Redville," said Kelly. "Winter lasts a long time here."

Next Duncan stopped at a kennel containing a black-and-tan German shepherd. The dog lunged at the window, barking and snarling. Duncan pulled back quickly and moved on.

"I guess," said Mia, "he didn't like that one."

"I know German shepherds can be really sweet and friendly," said Kelly. "But that dog looked mean. Or maybe just upset from being here."

Suddenly Duncan turned around and spotted the girls. He smiled and gestured for them to join him.

"Oh, no!" whispered Mia. "We've blown our cover. Ditch the notebook!"

"You sound like a real spy." Kelly laughed.

"Well, Perry watches a lot of those stupid spy movies with James Bond, so I just sort of picked up the lingo."

The girls hurried over to Duncan, trying to act normal. "Hey, Grandpa," said Kelly. "What's happening?"

"Just looking," he said. "How about you? And where's your dad, Kelly?"

"Oh, he went to look at cats," stammered Kelly. "Over there."

"He hates cats. They make him sneeze, don't they?"

"I guess so," said Kelly, giving Mia a pleading look.

"Actually, I think maybe he went to the bathroom," said Mia. "Have you seen any really great dogs yet?"

"Well, I did see one," Duncan replied. "Come over here and tell me what you think about this little guy."

The girls followed Duncan as he turned left and strode toward a small kennel at the end of a long row. There, curled up on the cement floor with a green spiky ball between his front paws, was a fluffy white dog. The minute he noticed them, the dog sat up and wagged his tail.

"Oh, he's adorable," cooed Mia. "Look at him!"

"Ohhhh," whispered Kelly, completely enchanted. "What kind is he?"

"Says here," Duncan read from the posted card, "that he's a West Highland terrier, or a Westie."

"Westie?" Kelly repeated. "I've never heard of them."

"I have," Duncan said with a smile. "They come from the same place in Scotland that I did as a boy."

"You came from Scotland?" asked Mia. "Cool!"

"I was born there," Duncan explained. "But my family moved to California when I was five. My uncle had already moved there, and he needed some help with his strawberry farm. I don't remember too much about growing up in Scotland, but the times I've traveled back, I do feel some sort of strange pull. As if I've come home."

"That means," Mia observed, "that Kelly's part Scottish."

"That's right," said Duncan. "She has the same fair, freckled skin of all her ancestors."

But Kelly barely heard him. She was mesmerized by the white dog. He was small and low to the ground, with a sweet, shaggy face, dark eyes, tiny ears, and a pert black nose. He stared back at Kelly, wagging his tail and sniffing the air. To Kelly, the dog seemed friendly, alert, and very vivacious. He didn't act mean or upset like some dogs in the shelter, nor sad and withdrawn like others.

Sandy
Pug

Scottie
West Highland
Terrier

"You like this fellow?" Duncan asked.

"He's wonderful!" said Kelly. "It says his name is Scottie."

"A good Scottish name. You know, I believe these dogs were originally raised to hunt foxes and badgers."

"But they're so tiny," said Mia.

"But tough, too," Duncan said. "I never owned one, but I've heard great things about them. I wonder how Mr. Scottie here got himself stranded in a shelter for the holidays."

"Do you think he ran away?" Kelly wondered. "No one would abandon a dog as wonderful as this!"

"I don't know," said Duncan, shaking his head. "I bet there's a story to be told for every animal in this place. And I'd certainly like to hear the story of this cute fellow."

Suddenly, Kelly knew! She knew in her heart that Scottie was the dog she wanted to give to her grandpa. She could tell that Duncan liked the dog. Scottie was cute, funny, friendly — and best of all, he was Scottish like Duncan! It was perfect! She couldn't wait to tell her dad that she had found a dog that would have some personal meaning to Grandpa!

Just then a strange look came over Duncan's face. "Excuse me," he said. "I'll be right back. I just need to — I have to — I'll see you in a few minutes."

"Is he all right?" Mia asked as Duncan disappeared around the corner.

"I think so. Maybe he needed to use the bathroom. He's kind of modest about things like that."

"Oh," said Mia. "So, spy girl, what do you think so far?"

"I think that this is the one. Scottie is the dog I want to get my grandpa for Christmas."

"I was afraid you were going to say that," said Mia.

"Why?" asked Kelly. "Don't you like him?"

"I love him! But look." Mia pointed to an orange sticker near the top left-hand corner of the window.

The sticker read, I'VE BEEN ADOPTED!

"No!" cried Kelly. "Why didn't we notice that before?"

"I guess because we were so busy falling in love with Scottie," Mia answered sadly.

Kelly felt as though her heart were breaking. It wasn't supposed to happen this way. She put her nose against the window and gazed longingly at Scottie, who reached a paw up to the glass.

"I hope," said Kelly to the dog, "that you're going to as good a home as we would have given you. Merry Christmas, Scottie."

FIVE

Meeting Mrs. Gibson

"Boy," said Perry, "this dog lady lives way out in the boonies!"

"Thanks for taking us," said Kelly from the backseat of Perry's old red Jeep. "You're really helping us out."

"No problem." Perry smiled at Kelly in his rearview mirror. "It's the holiday season and I want Santa to be good to me this year. Your parents are busy grading papers, our mom is busy making Christmas ornaments, so I'm the designated driver for Kelly-Belly and Mia-Sophia!"

Mia looked up from the map she was studying. "Perr, you need to take a right at the next stop sign, then proceed for three quarters of a mile on the dirt road."

"You're an excellent navigator for a little kid," Perry said, bringing the Jeep to a full stop. He fiddled with the radio, which hardly ever worked. The only station he could find was one with a woman singing high-pitched opera in Italian. "Oh, linguine and spaga-tini, and spu-moni for me and Tony!" he crooned in a fake opera voice.

Kelly and Mia cracked up, even though they knew all his jokes and antics by now. Perry always made up weird lyrics to songs on the radio.

As the Jeep bumped along, Kelly looked out the window. She studied the snowy landscape dotted by tall green pines and the empty cornfields rutted with ice. Then she looked down at the card in her hand. In small black script it read: VIRGINIA GIBSON, BREEDER, WEST HIGHLAND TERRIERS. TWENTY-THREE MILL POND ROAD.

Her heart beat fast with anticipation — and a touch of worry. On the phone, Mrs. Gibson had sounded very stern. Yes, she had some puppies, but she wasn't inclined to sell them impulsively to little girls for Christmas presents.

"It's serious business," she'd said, "to bring a dog into your life. I'll need to talk with you and interview you. Can you come on Friday?"

"Yes!" Kelly had told her. Crossing her fingers, she thought, *Please, please have a Westie for me to give to Grandpa!*

"Now, how did you find this breeder?" Perry asked, turning onto a long gravel driveway. "The yellow pages?"

"No," Mia explained as she carefully folded her map. "After Kelly found out that the Westie she wanted at the animal shelter was already adopted, a volunteer told her about this woman out in the country who breeds them."

"A stroke of good luck," declared Perry.

"I hope so," Kelly sighed. "She sounded a little scary on the phone."

"I'll protect you," Perry promised. "Come on, ladies, let's go meet Mrs. Bestie-Westie."

Kelly felt her hand tremble as she rang the doorbell of the yellow Victorian-style house with red trim and a red door.

"It's a gingerbread house," said Mia, looking up over her head at the intricate woodwork.

"And don't forget," added Perry with a wink, "who lives in the gingerbread house — the wicked witch who eats little girls!"

Just then the door opened and an attractive woman with short brown hair and bright red lipstick smiled out at them. She looked older than Kelly's parents but not as old as Grandpa. "Hello," she said in a pleasant voice. "You found the house all right?"

"No problem," said Perry, holding out his hand to Mrs. Gibson. "I'm Perry, and this is my sister, Mia, and our friend Kelly."

"So, you're Kelly!" said Mrs. Gibson. "Well, come on in. It's freezing outside."

Everyone followed Mrs. Gibson inside and down a hallway which led to a large, warm family room. A fire glowed in the fireplace, and Christmas carols played softly. "Sit down," said Mrs. Gibson. "Make yourselves at home. I'm just going to get my files and a pen."

As she left the room, Perry looked at the girls and grinned. "She doesn't seem like a witch," he said. "I don't think witches wear much lipstick."

"But where are the dogs?" whispered Mia.

"I don't know," Kelly answered, looking around. "I can't wait to see them!"

"Okay," said Mrs. Gibson, returning with a fat pile of papers. "Here we go. Kelly, may I ask you a few questions?" She sat down near the fire and tucked her feet up comfortably in the chair.

"Sure," said Kelly, her eyes wide with anticipation.

"You said on the phone you wanted to buy a Westie puppy for your grandfather. Is that right?"

"Right. For Christmas."

"Tell me, Kelly, does your grandfather know about this?"

Kelly shook her head. "No, it's a surprise."

"Why a Westie, Kelly?"

Kelly took a deep breath and looked at Mia for support. "Well, for one thing, my grandpa is from Scotland. And for another thing, when we visited the animal shelter, he really liked the Westie we saw there."

"Do you know much about the breed?"

"Mia and I did some research," said Kelly. "We found a book at the library. We know they were first bred as hunters in Scotland."

"By Colonel Edward Donald Malcolm," added Mia.

"Very good!" Mrs. Gibson laughed. "I'm impressed so far."

"And," continued Kelly, "they make great companions, which is what I want for my grandpa. And they love the outdoors but are also happy inside."

"And," said Mia, "they are loving and loyal, but they're not wimps! They have their own minds."

"Oh, is that ever true," agreed Mrs. Gibson. "They have terrific self-esteem! There is an old saying about Westies that they are small dogs who think they are big dogs!"

Perry laughed at this and asked, "So, when do

we get to meet these awesome creatures?"

"Not quite yet," said Mrs. Gibson, becoming more serious. "A few more questions. Kelly, how serious are you about bringing a dog into your life? Do you understand what's involved? And what if your grandfather isn't quite as excited by the gift as you are?"

"I've thought about that," Kelly admitted. "And so have my mom and dad. But my grandpa has had dogs all his life. He loves them as much as I do. Only, my grandma died a few years ago and he moved from California to live with us. And I think it would make him happy to have a dog as a companion when I'm at school and my parents are at work."

"What kind of yard do you have?"

"It's fairly small," said Kelly. "But it's fenced. And it has nice shade trees and good places to sniff around."

"Would you or your grandfather take the dog out on a leash for a walk every day?" asked Mrs. Gibson. "They need regular exercise."

"Oh, yes!" cried Kelly.

"Don't worry about that," Perry put in. "Kelly loves dogs. I think she loves our two dogs more than we do sometimes."

"Well," said Mrs. Gibson. "You seem like a nice girl, Kelly, and you've certainly done your research, which is more than many adults are willing to do before picking out a dog. But I want to phone your parents this evening and check things out with them — especially the financial arrangements. Would that be all right with you?"

"Sure." Kelly nodded. "But you don't have to worry about the money. I've been saving for a bike for a long time. The money is in my savings account at the bank."

Mrs. Gibson regarded Kelly thoughtfully. "You're willing to forego a new bicycle in order to buy a dog for your grandfather?"

Kelly nodded, unsure of what else to say.

"Well, would you like to meet the puppies, then?" asked Mrs. Gibson, rising gracefully from her chair.

"Yes!" said Kelly, Mia, and Perry in unison.

"Follow me, then." Mrs. Gibson led them to a light-filled room off the kitchen. The floor was covered with shiny linoleum, and a pen was set up in a stop-sign shape. In the center of this, in a heap of soft blankets, were four tiny, fluffy Westie puppies.

"Four of them!" exclaimed Mia. "Look how cute."

"Yes," said Mrs. Gibson. "Westies have small litters. There are two males and two females in this litter."

"They are *beautiful*!" said Kelly.

"Pretty cute!" agreed Perry.

"I think so," said Mrs. Gibson. She reached inside the pen and picked up a puppy. "This," she said, "is Constance. Over in the corner there is her brother Phelps. They're already spoken for — they'll become show dogs."

"What does that mean?" asked Perry.

"It means that the owners will raise them to

compete in shows with other Westies. They're judged by a complete set of standard breed characteristics."

"And who are the other two?" asked Kelly. She was already drawn to the one enthusiastically playing with a small stuffed bear.

"Well, the one chewing the bear is Oscar. And the one fast asleep is Sophie. Those are the two available puppies from this litter."

"Can we see Oscar?" asked Kelly. She wanted desperately to hold the puppy, but she was determined to be patient.

Mrs. Gibson leaned down and scooped Oscar up into her arms. "He's a gem," she said. "Very alert and friendly. Very intelligent. And quite a distinct personality."

"Can I — can I hold him?" Kelly asked. "If that's all right?"

"Of course!" said Mrs. Gibson, handing him carefully to Kelly.

Oscar immediately licked Kelly on the nose,

his small tail wagging. While Kelly held him, Mrs. Gibson explained what made Oscar an especially nice Westie.

"See how healthy and pink his skin is beneath the fur?" she said. "And he has a solid black nose, black eye rims, and all black claws and pads on his feet."

Mia and Perry both stroked Oscar, too, and Oscar seemed to thrive on the attention. Kelly held him close and smelled him, remembering that the library book had said that Westies didn't have the usual "doggie smell." It was true! To Kelly, he just smelled new and sweet.

"How old are they?" asked Perry.

"About eleven weeks. They won't be ready to leave here for another two or three weeks."

"Why is that?" asked Kelly, silently calculating that two weeks would be just in time for Christmas.

"You don't want them to leave until they've lost all their baby teeth and lost their soft puppy coat. You want to be sure they've been checked out by a veterinarian, and that they're ready to bond with a new person and leave their litter mates."

"Is Oscar going to be ready? May I have him?" asked Kelly. She held her breath as she waited for Mrs. Gibson's reply.

"I think it's very possible," Mrs. Gibson said, smiling. "But as I mentioned, I want to talk to your parents. And you would need to come back several more times before you could take him."

"Why?" asked Mia. "When we adopted Bo and Chubby, we brought them home with us that very same day."

"Well," explained Mrs. Gibson, "as the breeder, I invest a lot of time, money, and love in these puppies. I feel responsible for their futures — I want to know where they're going, and that they'll be given good care. I would want to show Kelly how to care for Oscar, and give her his registration papers, and talk about the transition to a new home, and what kind of equipment is needed. There's a lot more to this than meets the eye."

"I guess so!" said Perry. "I think it's cool that you're so responsible."

"Thank you!" said Mrs. Gibson. "I think it's cool that the three of you are pursuing this in such a well-thought-out way. You wouldn't believe how many calls I get this time of year from people who think that a white dog with a red bow sitting under a green tree would make a lovely holiday picture. They don't think about the big picture — the day-to-day care and love involved in bringing an animal into your life."

Kelly hugged Oscar close and then looked at Mrs. Gibson very seriously. "I know I told you I wanted Oscar to give to my grandpa for Christmas. But if he's not ready, or you think we need more time, then I don't care about the Christmas part. I just want Oscar to be with Grandpa Dunc."

"Well," said Mrs. Gibson, "let me talk to your parents tonight. Will they be at home?"

"Yes," said Kelly. "I think we're putting up our Christmas tree."

"Good, then we'll talk tonight. Can you find your way back to town?"

"I think so," Perry answered. "I have Mia-Sophia here to navigate."

"Well, then, let me show you out. I think it's really starting to snow now."

"Wait," said Kelly as she reluctantly handed Oscar back to Mrs. Gibson. "What about Sophie? What will happen to her?"

"Oh, don't worry about her," said Mrs. Gibson. "I've already had several calls, and I'm expecting someone later today who's interested in a female."

Kelly gave Oscar a gentle kiss on the top of his head. "Good-bye!" she whispered. "I hope I see you soon!"

Oscar gave a short, friendly bark in response, his tail wagging furiously. When Mrs. Gibson put him down inside the wire mesh enclosure, Oscar ran right back to his teddy bear.

You and Grandpa Dunc are meant to be together! Kelly thought as she gave the puppy one more wave good-bye.

SIX

Mysterious Grandpa Dunc

"Two more days until winter break!" exclaimed Kelly, bouncing on the bottom bunk of Mia's bed.

"One more day until the school play." Mia looked down at Kelly from the top bunk.

"And eight more days until Oscar comes home with me!" said Kelly.

The two girls laughed and shouted until the bed shook against the wall. Then a knock sounded at Mia's bedroom door.

"Come in," invited Mia, sitting up on her bed. Perry poked his head inside the door.

"What's going on in here? An earthquake or something?"

"Nope!" Kelly laughed. "We're just excited about Oscar!"

"So the dog lady said you could have the little cotton ball, after all," teased Perry. "There goes the neighborhood — Oscar the Scottish Laird among the likes of Bo and Chubby!"

"Oscar will love Bo and Chubby," protested Mia, and right on cue the two dogs wandered into the room. Bo ambled over to Kelly, licking her outstretched hand.

"I'll always love you," Kelly told the dogs, "even when Oscar comes. You were the first dogs in my life."

Chubby flopped to the floor with a sigh, while Bo sniffed a dirty purple sock he found under the bed.

"So, when do you pick up the puff ball, and do you think your grandpa has a clue?" asked Perry. He was munching on a green apple, taking loud, smacking bites.

"We pick him up the day before Christmas," Kelly replied. "I have to buy a bunch of stuff — like a travel kennel, a leash, food — first."

"Do you think your grandpa knows?" Mia lowered herself down from the top bunk to pet Chubby.

Kelly sighed and looked at Mia. "I don't think so but I'm a little worried."

"Why?" asked Perry.

"Well, he's been acting kind of strange," Kelly explained. "It seems as if he's never home, and when I ask him about his day, he doesn't say much. He just gives me this goofy smile."

"Hey," exclaimed Mia, "that sounds exactly like the way Perry acts when he has a new girlfriend!"

"Yuck!" Kelly laughed. "I don't think my grandpa has a girlfriend."

"Wait a minute," said Perry, "don't be so sure. You think just because the guy's old he can't have a sweetheart? He's a great guy — smart, charming, and not bad-looking for a man his age."

Kelly looked at Mia, rolling her eyes. She was used to Perry's jokes and weird ideas. But Mia wasn't laughing. Her eyes were closed.

"I can picture it," Mia said. "I can see your

grandpa meeting some really cool lady. That's what happened to our grandma, right, Perry?"

"Right!" said Perry. "She was a widow for a long, long time. But then she met this guy at a square dance, and they've lived happily ever after. They're probably do-si-do-ing right this minute in the suburbs of Chicago."

"But where would my grandpa meet someone?" asked Kelly. "He doesn't square-dance. He never has anyone over. He just drives around looking for antiques."

Mia stood up and brushed dog hair from her jeans. "Remember, he hasn't been home much, and he doesn't like to tell you where he's been."

"I can't imagine him with someone who's not my grandma," Kelly said a little sadly.

"But life must go on," Perry added gently. "You wouldn't like him to be alone for the rest of his life, I bet."

"No," Kelly agreed, "but what if it's true? What if he's . . . dating someone! Maybe he'll be too busy to have a dog. Maybe he won't want Oscar!"

"Nah," said Perry cheerfully. "Who wouldn't want Oscar? He's awesome! Listen, Kelly-Belly, don't worry! It's going to be a great surprise."

"Right!" Mia said. "Don't worry. Maybe your grandpa has just been out Christmas shopping and he doesn't want you to know what he's getting you."

"He always gives me money for Christmas," said Kelly.

"Speaking of money," said Perry. "I have to drive into town to go to the bank. Want to come?"

"Sure!" shouted Mia. "Want to, Kelly?"

"Do you think I could go to the pet store near the bank and buy a leash?"

"No problem," said Perry. "I'll go up and tell Mom."

An hour later, just as she was leaving the pet store, Kelly ran smack into Grandpa Dunc. They collided outside the door and nearly knocked each other over.

"Grandpa!" cried Kelly. "Are you all right?"

"Fine, fine." He laughed, straightening his hat. "What in the world are you up to?"

Kelly had a moment of panic, completely unsure what to say. There she was, holding a yellow plastic bag from the pet store containing a new leash and collar for Oscar!

"Um," Kelly stammered, "I was just — we were just —"

Perry saved the day, grabbing the bag from Kelly. "Hey, Duncan," he said cheerfully. "Kelly-Belly and Mia-Sophia were just helping me pick out a gift for Bo, our dog." Perry pulled the red collar out of the bag and held it up for Duncan to see. "What do you think?"

"Nice. And a lucky dog to get a Christmas gift."

"Oh, we have stockings for both our dogs," Mia explained, nudging Kelly with her boot. "They're part of our family."

"That's just as it should be." Duncan nodded. "When I had dogs, it was the same way."

"Do you miss having them?" Perry asked in-

nocently. Mia and Kelly held their breath.

"Sure," Duncan admitted. "Of course, my life is different now."

Kelly wondered what he meant by different. Did he mean different because he was a widower, or different because he didn't live in California? Or did he mean different because — he had a girl-friend?

"What are *you* up to?" Kelly asked Duncan.

Duncan shrugged his shoulders and smiled at Kelly. "Oh, you know — a little of this, a little of that. Some errands . . ."

"Oh," said Kelly. "So, I guess I'll see you for dinner, then."

"Actually, honey, I won't be home for dinner. Will you let your mom know that I have a — an appointment?"

"Sure." Kelly smiled, trying to act casual. "But you are coming to our holiday play at school to-morrow night, aren't you?"

"Wouldn't miss it!" Duncan gave Kelly a kiss on the head.

Kelly, Mia, and Perry watched Duncan turn around and head north on Main Street, his hands in his pockets, whistling a tune as he walked.

"He sure seems happy," Perry noted. "Maybe he does have a lady friend."

"I wish I knew," sighed Kelly. "Suddenly, getting him a dog seems very risky."

"Life is risky," said Perry in his upbeat voice. "Want to get some hot chocolate at the Dairy Barn?"

"I think we should follow him," said Kelly, forming a plan in her mind. "Let's see where he goes. If we hurry, we can catch up."

"Just like your James Bond movies, Perry," said Mia.

"Cool! Follow me, and be quiet. If he sees us, we're on our way to the Dairy Barn, okay?"

"Okay!" Kelly and Mia agreed.

Silently, the three hurried up Main Street, weaving in and out of groups of students and holiday shoppers clogging the sidewalks. The windows of the shops were decorated with lights, green garlands, and ribbons. A university choir sang Christmas carols from the steps of the town hall. Kelly ignored all this, intent on locating Grandpa Dunc.

"I see him!" whispered Perry. "I think he's heading for Cuts Are Us!"

"He must be getting his hair cut," said Kelly, relief in her voice.

"That seems pretty harmless," said Mia. "I don't think you go out on a date to Cuts Are Us."

"Maybe he's getting ready for a date," Perry said. "A shave, a haircut, a little spicy cologne! That old tiger!"

"Gross!" said Mia and Kelly together. "No way."

"Stop!" commanded Perry. They stood one store from the hair shop, waiting for Perry to divulge his James Bond plan.

"Here's the thing," he said to the girls. "I'll put on my sunglasses and walk casually by. You wait here. If there's any action, I'll signal for you to come, okay?"

"Okay," they agreed.

Perry put on his black wraparound glasses and pulled the collar of his parka up around his neck.

"You still look like yourself." Mia giggled.

"Hush," whispered Perry. "I'm a secret agent in disguise. I can walk the world unnoticed."

"Right," said Mia, rolling her eyes.

Perry strolled up to the window of Cuts Are Us and peeked in, while Mia and Kelly waited breathlessly. After a moment, he signaled the girls to approach.

Kelly couldn't believe her eyes when she looked through the shiny glass window. There in a shampoo chair sat Duncan, a plastic cape around his neck. He was leaning back into the sink, while a woman who looked a bit younger than him massaged his soapy head. They both were laughing and talking. To Kelly, Duncan looked extremely happy.

"I can't believe it!" said Mia. "Look at that!"

"He's just getting his hair washed," said Perry. "No reason to panic."

But just then, Duncan sat up from the sink. The woman wrapped a towel around his head, and then leaned down to whisper something in his ear. She and Duncan laughed some more, then Duncan stood up and reached for her hand, shaking it and bowing low. This was followed by more laughter and the woman pretending to curtsy.

"A younger woman," Perry commented. "And very nice-looking!"

"I can't believe this," said Kelly. "It's really true! Look at them!"

"Now, now," said Perry, "don't jump to conclusions. They could be just friends goofing off together."

"Yeah," said Mia, "it's not like they're kissing or anything."

"Kissing! Gross!" teased Perry. "Not kissing!"

"And remember," said Kelly, "he said he had an *appointment* tonight!"

"Oops," said Perry, giving the girls a gentle shove. "They're moving this way. Let's go."

The three hurried past the window and came to

a stop in front of a dry cleaner store. Perry took Kelly's hand and patted it. "Kelly-Belly, I don't think you should make a big deal of this. There's really nothing to know yet, and your grandpa might feel betrayed if he found out we were spying on him."

"True," said Kelly. "It's his life, after all. Only — only —"

"What?" asked Mia.

"Well, what if it's true that my grandpa is dating her? What if they fall in love and get married and he moves away? Or she moves in with him?"

"Then you'd have a new grandma who can cut hair!" said Perry, giving Kelly a thumbs-up. "She could probably show you guys how to do all kinds of fancy braids and stuff!"

Kelly smiled at Perry. He was so nice! He always cracked jokes and tried to make people feel better. Kelly thought teenagers got a lot of bad publicity, because Perry was a model brother and friend.

"But what if he got so busy that he didn't want

a dog to take care of? Remember, I'm giving him Oscar as a friend and companion."

"People can have lots of different kinds of friends, Kelly," Perry said.

"But what if his life is changing and it doesn't include animals?" added Kelly. "I feel as if I might be making a big mistake. Maybe I should have just gotten him a sweater or something."

"It'll be okay," said Mia, trying to comfort her friend. "Don't think about that — just keep thinking about Oscar. Think about his cute face, and his little black nose, and his tail wagging — "

"You're right," said Kelly, forming a picture in her mind of the small, friendly white dog. Thinking about Oscar made her feel a little bit better.

But she had an overwhelming desire to peek in Cuts Are Us one more time. So, Kelly walked carefully back to the edge of the window and peered in. What she saw sent a shiver down her spine.

There was Grandpa Dunc, pulling a small

wrapped package out of the pocket of his coat and handing it ceremoniously to the woman who'd washed his hair.

Not wanting to see anything more, Kelly ran away as fast as she could.

SEVEN

Another Visit to Oscar

On her second visit to the Westie breeder, Kelly giggled as Oscar stood up in her lap and planted a kiss on her face. His curious eyes watched her every movement, and his ever-wagging tail flicked back and forth. Kelly smoothed the long white hair on either side of his nose and then petted the soft fur on his back. She looked up at her mother expectantly.

"So, what do you think, Mom?"

"He's everything you described and more!" Laura reached down to touch Oscar's soft, perky ears. "I think Grandpa will find him as irresistible as you do!"

"You know," said Mrs. Gibson to Laura, "this is quite an unusual situation. I've had people buy dogs for children and grandchildren, but never the other way around."

"Well," explained Laura, "Kelly has always done things that surprised us — ever since she was born!"

"And you believe that your father will be excited about having Oscar?" Mrs. Gibson continued talking to Laura while Kelly romped with the puppy.

"As I told you on the phone," Laura said, "my father loves dogs. He's always had at least one, if not two. I think this could be one of the best gifts he's ever received. The timing is very good."

Kelly listened to her mom and Mrs. Gibson visit and tried not to think about Grandpa Dunc and the woman at Cuts Are Us. She wanted her surprise to come off perfectly. She couldn't bear the thought that Grandpa Dunc might be preparing to embark on a new chapter of his life — one that maybe wouldn't include Oscar, or her! She wanted to tell her mom about the woman, and about the gift and

the laughing, but she didn't want to admit that she had spied on Grandpa Dunc.

Mrs. Gibson's smooth voice interrupted her thoughts. "I've showed Kelly how to take care of Oscar's coat, and how to bathe him. We've talked about food, and shots, and I've recommended a veterinarian. Do you have any other questions?"

Laura thought for a moment, then smiled and shook her head. "I think we're ready. We're going to pick up the travel crate tomorrow, and Kelly has already bought the leash and collar and ordered the identification tag."

"So, then — you're set for December twenty-fourth to take him home!" announced Mrs. Gibson.

Kelly hugged Oscar close to her and whispered, "That's only six days from now! Then you'll be part of our family!"

Oscar gave a quick, high bark, as though he understood Kelly completely.

"Why don't I give you Oscar's registration today, and that will be one less thing to worry about on the twenty-fourth." Mrs. Gibson opened her file and took out a piece of paper, which she handed ceremoniously to Laura.

"You should put this in Grandpa's stocking," Laura said to Kelly. "He'll want to keep it with Oscar's medical information."

"This is so exciting!" Kelly exclaimed.

Just then, Oscar sprang from her lap and trotted down the hall.

"Where's he off to?" Kelly asked.

"Probably in search of Sophie," laughed Mrs. Gibson.

"Who is Sophie?" asked Laura.

"That's Oscar's sister," Kelly explained. "She's as cute as he is, but a little more — well —"

"Relaxed," supplied Mrs. Gibson. "She's not quite as adventurous as Oscar."

"I thought Grandpa would like a more active dog," Kelly said, "since he's pretty active himself."

"Good choice," agreed Laura. "They'll wear each other out."

"By the way," Kelly asked Mrs. Gibson, "did someone adopt Sophie?"

"Oh, yes. Sophie is going to have a nice home, too, I think. Another Christmas puppy!"

"I'm glad! It's kind of sad that they won't be together, but I'm happy they'll both have good homes. I did have this fantasy that Mia would adopt Sophie, but her mom said two dogs were enough."

"I have to agree with her," laughed Laura. "You two girls are canine crazy!"

"That's how I was as a young girl," said Mrs. Gibson, "and look at me now! Surrounded by dogs and litters of puppies!"

"A perfect life," sighed Kelly.

"We should go, honey," Laura told her daughter. "It's getting late."

"Oscar!" called Mrs. Gibson. "Come say good-bye!"

Oscar wiggled back into the room and sat at Kelly's feet. She picked him up and gave him a kiss. "See you in six days," she told him.

"Oh, wait a minute," said Mrs. Gibson, "I think that's Sophie." She reached for the dog and quickly checked him over. "Yes, this is Sophie."

"I can't believe I didn't know!" said Kelly. "They look exactly alike!"

"*Almost* exactly." Mrs. Gibson laughed. "They have a few defining differences!"

Laura and Kelly giggled about the mix-up all the way home. And Kelly almost forgot about the woman from Cuts Are Us.

But at the holiday program that night, Kelly's worries came rushing back.

Standing on the stage, Kelly could see her mom and dad trying to find seats in the crowded auditorium. Grandpa Dunc followed closely behind them, smiling at people as he passed them, holding his hat in his hand. It made Kelly feel warm inside to see the three of them together — her family and her fans!

But then she noticed Duncan stopping to wave

at someone behind him. "Look!" hissed Kelly, grabbing Mia's arm. "It's her! The Cuts Are Us woman!"

"Wow!" Mia whistled. "It *is* her! What's she doing here?"

"Do you think Grandpa invited her?" Kelly asked. Her voice was trembling, and she felt funny inside.

"I don't know," Mia admitted. "Pretty weird."

"She's coming with him!" Kelly reported. "She's sitting with him and my mom and dad! I can't believe it!"

"We'll try to find out more after the show," Mia consoled. "Don't worry. She looks pretty nice."

"I know," Kelly admitted. "She probably *is* nice. And I'm glad he has a friend. But what if he doesn't have time for Oscar?"

Just then, the music teacher signaled for everyone to be quiet, and the holiday program began. Kelly watched as her dad aimed his video camera toward the stage and adjusted the lens.

After the first- and second-graders presented

their musical number about Kwanzaa, and the third-graders sang about Hanukkah, it was time for the fourth grade to do their dance in honor of the Chinese New Year. The thirty girls and boys arranged themselves in a line as the teachers helped drape a gigantic piece of red silk over them. Two kids at the front of the line put on the ornate and fierce-looking puppet head, and the line became a moving, dancing dragon!

The audience went wild as the dragon snaked down the center aisle, past clapping parents and flashing cameras. From her vantage point near the back of the line, Kelly couldn't see much more than the feet of the kids in front of her. She kept her head down and concentrated on her footwork.

When the music ended, the dragon bowed and the audience cheered again. The students whipped off the red silk and took a final bow — this time as thirty sweaty, happy boys and girls. Kelly could see her parents applauding and laughing. And so were Grandpa Dunc and Ms. Cuts Are Us.

After the fifth-graders read Christmas poems and the sixth grade did a play about Mexico's Posada celebration, the program ended with the students and audience singing holiday carols together. And then it was time for punch, coffee, and cookies in the school gym. Kelly found Mia and made her promise to come along.

"Let's hurry out and try to find them," urged Kelly. "Before they get away!"

"Where would they go?" Mia laughed. "They're not escaped prisoners!"

"I know. But maybe they have plans for later."

"Okay," Mia agreed. "Let's be spies again."

In the gym, it took the girls a few minutes to find Kelly's family. First they ran into Mia's family, and Kelly had to stop and hug Joni, David, Ben, and Perry. Joni asked her all about Oscar, as Mia whispered something to Perry.

Perry took Kelly aside. "So, Sheila Shampoo showed up, huh?"

"Yeah," sighed Kelly. "We're trying to find them and spy some more."

"Need any help? I have my sunglasses with me."

"No," said Kelly. "But thanks for asking."

Finally, Kelly spotted her family, standing under one of the basketball hoops. "Look!" she said to Mia. "There they are!"

"Just act casual," whispered Mia, taking her friend's elbow and pulling her gently along. "Be cool."

"Here they are!" said Kelly's dad. "The Dragon Ladies!"

"You were wonderful!" said Laura. "I loved the dance!"

"Bravo!" said Grandpa Dunc, giving both girls a hug. "I can't wait to watch it again on the videotape."

"Thanks!" said Kelly. "It was fun."

"Kelly, I'd like you to meet a friend of mine," Duncan continued, turning to the woman at his left. "This is Celeste Freed. She cuts my hair, and she also has a grandchild at this school."

"Really?" asked Kelly, as calmly as possible. "What grade?"

"Second." Celeste had a rich, sweet voice. "Do you know Peter Freed?"

Kelly and Mia looked at each other and shook their heads. "I don't think so," said Kelly. "But the second-graders are at the other end of the building from us."

"I can't seem to locate him in this crowd," said Celeste. "I'd like to introduce you to him, and to my son and daughter-in-law, but I can't quite see them yet."

"We'll find them," Duncan said, smiling at Celeste.

We? thought Kelly. *Are they already a* we*?*

"If I know Peter," Celeste said with a laugh, "he's probably over at the cookie table. He's crazy about cookies."

"Well, so are these girls," said Laura. "Maybe we should all head over and try to find your family, Celeste."

"That's awfully kind," Celeste replied.

Kelly wondered if her mom knew that Duncan had given Celeste a present. And that the present had come in a small, square box — the kind that rings came in! She looked at Celeste's hands, but they were free of jewelry. She did have small blue earrings in her ears and a pin shaped like a Christmas tree on her coat collar. Could either of those have been the present Grandpa Dunc gave her?

Without really stopping to think, Kelly took a deep breath and looked at Celeste. "May I ask you a question?" she said.

"Sure, honey," answered Celeste. "Ask away."

"Do you like dogs?"

Mia kicked her hard, keeping a wide, fake smile stretched across her face.

Celeste looked surprised. So did Kelly's parents and her grandpa.

"What makes you ask?" said Duncan, eyeing his granddaughter with a strange expression.

"I don't know," sputtered Kelly. "It's just that, um, Mia and I were talking about dogs earlier, and how you could tell a lot about a person by knowing whether they like dogs or not."

"We're doing a paper on it for school," said Mia, trying to rescue her friend. "We're supposed to interview people besides our families — and well, you're a person, so —"

Celeste laughed and looked up at Duncan. "Fourth-graders are even more mysterious than second-graders!" To Kelly and Mia she said, "Yes, I do like dogs."

"You do?" Kelly said happily.

"Congratulations! I mean, that's great!" said Mia.

"But," Celeste continued, "I'm a little bit allergic to most animals. They make me sneeze."

Kelly tried hard to keep her face from falling into a devastated frown. "Allergic, huh?"

"Been that way all my life," said Celeste. "But for your report you can definitely say that I like dogs."

Kelly suddenly felt as if she was going to cry. She kept her eyes opened wide, so no tears would form. "Excuse me," she choked. "And thanks." Then she pushed her way through the crowd.

"Wait," cried Mia. "I'll come with you."

Out in the cool, empty hall, Kelly leaned against the drinking fountain and splashed some water on her face.

"Are you okay?" Mia asked.

"I guess so," said Kelly. "But don't you see? It's all ruined! My grandpa's in love with someone who's allergic to dogs! And just in time for his Christmas present, which happens to be a *dog*!"

EIGHT

The Storm

"Look at the snow!" Kelly exclaimed to her parents on the morning of Christmas Eve. "There must be six inches already!"

"It snowed all night," her dad confirmed, looking out the window and studying the vast, untouched whiteness of the backyard. "I listened to the radio earlier and they're predicting a real Midwest snowstorm."

"Where's Grandpa? Has he already had breakfast?"

"I'm not sure," said Laura, turning pancakes at the stove. "There's no path in the snow from the carriage house, so I'm guessing he hasn't been out yet."

"Dad, we have to pick up Oscar today," Kelly reminded. "Don't forget."

"Kelly, the State Patrol is already closing many of the country roads. I'm not entirely sure we can get out to Mrs. Gibson's place."

"We *have* to!" insisted Kelly. "Tomorrow is Christmas!"

"Shh!" warned Laura, nodding her head toward the carriage house. "Grandpa's coming!"

Kelly slid into a vacant kitchen chair and tried to compose her face into a cheerful, neutral expression. But inside, her heart was churning. She had come too far with her Christmas surprise to have it ruined by the snow! Not to mention the appearance on the scene of Celeste from Cuts Are Us. Kelly still hadn't had the chance to discuss her grandfather's new romance with her parents. And in the past week Grandpa Dunc had been gone from home even more than usual. But whenever Kelly asked him what he'd been up to, he just smiled mysteriously and said, "Oh, a little of this, a little of that."

"Merry Christmas Eve!" Duncan called as he

opened the kitchen door. His furry hat was dusted with snow, and his breath came out in puffs of steamy air. "Hey, pancakes!"

"Morning, Grandpa." Kelly smiled. "You sound very cheerful this morning."

"How can you not be cheerful on such a beautiful day? This is my first white Christmas in a good long time!"

"That's true," said Laura, bringing over a heaping platter of pancakes and setting them down in the middle of the table. "In California, we sometimes had a rainy Christmas."

"What are you up to today, Duncan?" John asked. "Hope you don't have to go anywhere."

"Matter of fact," Duncan answered, "I've already been out. I got up very early to make a quick visit to someone. My truck did pretty well on the main roads."

Visit to someone? Kelly thought. *Celeste?*

"The news reports haven't been too promising this morning," John continued. "I'd recommend getting any other errands done right away. Then if we are snowed in, we can just enjoy a quiet Christmas Eve in front of the fire."

"I'm glad I went grocery shopping yesterday," said Laura. "I don't want to go out in this mess."

"Dad," Kelly said lightly, "speaking of going out, shouldn't we go pick up Mia and do our last errand?"

"Oh, honey," Laura said, "I just remembered! Mia's mom called to say that Mia has a cold. Joni doesn't want her going out today, but she'll see you tonight for Christmas Eve dinner."

Kelly tried to hide her disappointment, but a stray tear blinked out of the corner of one eye. Things were not going well at all. The strain of trying to keep Oscar a secret, combined with all the worry of whether or not getting a dog for Grandpa was the right thing to do — well, it was starting to make Kelly feel a little crazy.

John noticed Kelly's trembling mouth and patted her hand. "Go get dressed, Kelly, and let's try to run that errand."

"Would you like a ride?" Duncan asked helpfully.

"Um, no thanks," answered John quickly. "You know — Christmas surprises and all."

Duncan laughed as though this were the funniest joke he had ever heard. "Boy, do I ever know about that!" he said and laughed until his eyes watered.

Kelly wondered if her grandpa's fit of silliness had anything to do with keeping Celeste a secret. And if so, when did he plan to share his news with his family?

Too many secrets! she thought.

Though Kelly's father was an excellent winter driver, the journey to Mrs. Gibson's house was not easy. The roads were still open but barely passable. The snow seemed to be flying directly at the windshield, making it difficult to see the road ahead. Kelly kept quiet so her dad could concentrate and willed the car to arrive safely.

We're coming, Oscar! she thought over and

over. She smiled as she envisioned the happy, funny dog with his friendly dark eyes and perpetually wagging tail. She looked in the backseat at the travel kennel with the soft flannel blanket folded carefully inside and tried to imagine Oscar sitting there, his nose in the air, taking in everything he saw.

When they finally arrived at Mill Pond Road, Kelly was surprised to see a young woman she didn't recognize at the front door. "Hi," she said to Kelly. "I'm Liz! My mom said you'd be coming by."

"Oh," said Kelly. "You're her daughter from college?"

"Right." Liz smiled. "Home for the holidays. And you're here for Oscar, right?"

"Right!" said Kelly. "My dad's bringing in the kennel."

"Well," said Liz, "Mom said to tell you she's sorry she's not here, but she left very early this morning to pick up my brother from the airport and she hasn't made it back yet. I'm hoping they're not stranded."

"I know," Kelly agreed. "It's bad out there."

"Hang on and I'll go get Oscar. He's pretty excited today — it's as if he knows something's up."

Liz disappeared, leaving Kelly in the hallway. Her dad came in, carrying the small kennel, just as Liz returned with the prized Westie. He was wearing a red ribbon around his neck, looking just the way a Christmas dog should!

"Hey, Oscar!" Kelly called, her face breaking into a huge grin. "How are you, buddy? This is my dad, Oscar! Dad, meet Oscar."

John reached over and petted the puppy's head. "Pleased to meet you, Oscar. You're as white as all that snow out there."

Just then the dog shifted in her arms and Kelly gasped out loud. "Oh, no!" she cried. "Oops!"

"What's the matter?" asked John and Liz in unison.

"This isn't Oscar," Kelly explained. "Look — it's Sophie!"

Sure enough, the dog in Kelly's arms was definitely *not* a male dog. John looked confused, but

Liz's face went instantly pale. Her hand flew to cover her surprised mouth.

"Don't worry," Kelly said, laughing. "This happened the last time I was here. They look exactly alike. So, where's Oscar?"

Liz had difficulty finding her voice. "I can't believe I did this! I can't believe it!"

"What?" asked Kelly, starting to feel worried. "Is something wrong?"

"Kelly, I'm so sorry. I made a really terrible mistake! Mom told me to put a red ribbon on Oscar and a green one on Sophie. I must have mixed them up! Mom is going to kill me! But it was so early this morning — I hadn't even had a cup of coffee yet!"

"What are we going to do?" asked Kelly. "Is Oscar already gone?"

"Earlier," croaked Liz. "And with this weather, I don't know if we'll be able to straighten this mess out right away. I guess I could try to reach my mom on her portable phone."

"Wait a minute," said John. He sounded calm and reasonable, as if getting the wrong dog was no problem at all. "Kelly, why don't we just wait a day or two until Oscar is returned, and then we'll come over and pick him up. I'm sure Liz feels bad enough about the mix-up, and we don't need to have a bunch of people hurrying around on these icy roads."

No! thought Kelly. *Oscar can't be gone!* She hung her head. After all the planning, convincing, researching — after all the trips out to the country to learn about Oscar's care, and all the careful secret-keeping she'd done to make the surprise a real one for Duncan. She didn't want to cry in front of Liz, but the tears came anyway. She turned and buried her face in her father's green coat, gulping back a sob.

"Hey," said Liz, her voice full of kindness, "don't cry. Please don't cry!"

"She's had a long week or two keeping her secret," John explained.

"I know," said Liz. "Mom told me how excited

you've been about giving Oscar to your grandpa. She's been very impressed with how mature you are, and how loving you are with animals."

"Thanks," Kelly sniffed. "I think your mom's really great."

"I know!" Liz said, brightening suddenly. "Here's an idea. It's wacky, but it might be worth a try."

"What?" Kelly asked, wiping her eyes with her mittened hand.

"Well, what if you took Sophie? Just until tomorrow? I know she's not the right dog, but this way you'd at least have a dog to give your grandpa in the morning. Then we could make the exchange with the other people."

"But it wouldn't be the same as giving him Oscar."

"I think it just might work." John looked down at Kelly. "What do you think? It might make a pretty entertaining story to tell Grandpa."

Kelly stroked Sophie's soft fur, smiling despite herself. It would be funny to tell Grandpa Dunc all about the mix-up, and how Oscar and Sophie looked just alike.

"But what about the other people? Do they know they have the wrong dog yet?"

"I don't know," Liz admitted. "I don't know where to find their phone number. I'll have to wait until my mother gets back from the airport. But I do think you should take Sophie with you. I'll call you later, just as soon as Mom is home. We'll straighten it all out, I promise."

"Okay," Kelly sighed. "But I'm worried that the other people will come back today and want to have Sophie."

"I don't think that will happen," said John. "No sane person is going to head back out here in this storm. And I think we should get going, too, unless you want to spend Christmas Eve stuck in a ditch somewhere."

Kelly hugged Sophie to her. "Well, you *are* Oscar's sister, so you might as well come and spend Christmas with us." She helped her dad settle the puppy into the kennel, making sure to tuck the blanket around her.

"Again, I'm really sorry," Liz said. "But I promise, we'll straighten it out tomorrow."

"It's okay," said Kelly. "We'll take good care of Sophie, and when you talk to the other people, tell them to take good care of Oscar."

"I will," Liz promised. "And have a very Merry Christmas!"

A very weird Christmas, thought Kelly as they headed down the snowy front walk with Sophie nestled in her kennel.

On the way home, John sang softly along with the Christmas music on the radio. Kelly kept turning around to check on Sophie, who was sleeping soundly in her nest of blankets, her red ribbon looking festive against her white coat. She was cute — adorable even — but she just wasn't Oscar.

"Dad," began Kelly, trying to keep her voice

light, "do you think Grandpa will ever have a — you know — a girlfriend?"

"What makes you ask?" said John.

"I don't know." Kelly shrugged. "Just wondering."

"I think your grandpa would like that, Kelly, if he found a really nice woman who made him happy. It's been four years, and life does go on."

"I know," Kelly sighed. "But what if, for instance, he fell in love with someone who was allergic to dogs and that person couldn't be around Oscar?"

John shook his head and laughed at Kelly. "That's a lot of what-ifs!"

"But I want Grandpa to love Oscar as much as I do!"

"I think he will," John responded. "But, remember, from the very beginning we tried to make you understand that if the surprise backfired, Oscar would become your responsibility. And to tell you the truth, I don't think you'd mind it too much if Oscar were all yours!"

"If we ever get him back," Kelly sighed. "This whole thing has been so hard! Especially with Cel —" Kelly stopped herself before she finished saying the name of Grandpa's new friend.

"Sell what?" John asked.

"Oh, not *sell*," Kelly said quickly. "I mean *buying* a dog and trying to keep it a surprise."

"But I have to give you credit, Kelly. You had a wonderful, loving idea and you've carried it through with style. That's the true Christmas spirit."

"Thanks, Dad." Kelly felt like crying again, but this time because her heart was full and glad. Christmas was a magical time, if you could get past the hurry, and the craziness, and the things that didn't go just exactly as you'd planned.

John turned up the radio and sang, *"It's beginning to look a lot like Christmas, everywhere you go . . ."*

Kelly joined in, turning around to check on the sleeping Westie.

NINE

Christmas Eve

Kelly's mom met her at the back door, a worried expression on her face. "I'm so glad you're back!" she said. Her voice was full of relief, and the hug she gave Kelly was close and tight.

"The snow was really bad," Kelly explained, making way for her dad and the kennel. "It took forever to get home."

"I was trying not to worry," Laura said, "but the radio was reporting road closings and stranded motorists all over the place."

John closed the door behind him and set the kennel on the kitchen floor. He stamped his snow-caked boots and rubbed his hands together for warmth. "It was pretty bad," he told Laura, "but we stayed calm and sang Christmas carols, right, Kelly?"

"Right," said Kelly. She was already busy opening the latch of the kennel and bringing the sleepy puppy into her arms.

"Hello, Oscar!" Laura said, kneeling down. "Welcome home!"

"Mom," Kelly said with a laugh, "it's a long story, but this isn't Oscar!"

Laura looked confused. "It's not? Then who is it?"

"Her name is Sophie," John explained, "and she happens to be the sister of Oscar. There's been a little canine confusion today."

Kelly explained the whole story to Laura as Sophie explored the kitchen. She sniffed under the stove, ventured near a potted plant by the window, and barked at the broom leaning against the pantry door.

"So, let me get this straight," said Laura slowly. "Oscar is with another family right now — the

family who actually adopted Sophie. And we have Sophie, until we can get Oscar back. Which means that Grandpa is going to get Sophie for Christmas, but Oscar later on?"

"You got it!" Kelly said. "Pretty strange Christmas, huh?"

"And getting stranger by the minute. Right before you came home, Grandpa finally made it back. I stood here at the window and watched him bring three huge boxes into the carriage house. I wonder what he's up to!"

"I don't know," John said with a laugh, "but knowing Duncan, he'll have a great story to tell us tomorrow morning."

And, thought Kelly, *maybe he'll finally tell us about Celeste, who's allergic to dogs, and about the ring he gave her the other day!*

"Hey," she said aloud, suddenly looking around, "where'd Sophie go? Sophie! Sophie!" Kelly hurried out of the kitchen, calling for the dog. She wasn't in the dining room, she wasn't checking out the Christmas tree in the living room, and she wasn't in the downstairs study.

"Where are you, Sophie?" Kelly called, taking the stairs two at a time. She finally found the puppy sniffing the new dog bed she'd bought for Oscar. It was round and fluffy and covered in a washable plaid fabric. Sophie circled it several times, still sniffing, and then finally pulled herself up and collapsed in the middle.

Kelly laughed and moved over to pet Sophie. "Hey," she cooed, "don't get too comfortable, now. This bed is for Oscar to sleep in at Grandpa's house. You have to go to your real home in a couple of days."

Sophie looked up at Kelly. In her dark shining eyes was an expression of complete contentment. She rolled over and Kelly stroked her soft belly. "I hope you're going to a good family," she told Sophie, "because you're awfully sweet. And I hope with all my heart that Grandpa Dunc will be happy about this gift."

Sophie closed her eyes and sighed, burrowing into the soft bed. She was just a puppy — she didn't have to worry about complicated things like surprises and holidays and relationships between people.

"You're a lot more mellow than Oscar," Kelly noted. "I think wherever Oscar is right now, he's probably running around like crazy, exploring everything."

Kelly watched Sophie sleep for a few minutes, then tiptoed out of the room, closing the door behind her.

In the kitchen, Laura was holding the phone to her ear and staring anxiously out the back window.

"What's wrong?" Kelly asked.

"I'm trying to reach Grandpa, but he won't pick up the phone."

"Maybe he's sleeping."

"But he just got home," Laura said.

"Maybe he's taking a shower."

"Honey," said Laura, "would you do me a favor? Would you put on your coat and run over and just see if he's all right? He's been acting so strange today."

Because of Celeste! Kelly thought, but she didn't say it out loud. She was determined not to spoil her grandpa's secret, even though she was bursting to talk to her parents about the woman from Cuts Are Us.

"Okay," Kelly agreed, reaching for her coat. "Sophie's asleep, but keep your ears open in case she wakes up and misses me."

The wind almost knocked Kelly over as she opened the door and stepped into the backyard. The snow was falling thick and fast. Even though John had shoveled the driveway and walks early in the morning, they were covered once again. Her head down, Kelly lifted the heavy brass knocker on the door of the carriage house.

No one answered. Kelly knocked again. And again.

Finally, she heard her grandpa's voice calling, "I'm coming, I'm coming."

Kelly shivered, then did a little dance to try and keep warm.

The carriage door creaked open and Duncan's face peered out.

"Kelly!" he said, sounding surprised. "What are you doing out in this blizzard?"

"Mom was worried. You didn't answer the phone."

"Oh," said Duncan. "I must have been in the shower."

"That's what I told her," Kelly said, laughing. "She's being a worrywart today." But Kelly couldn't help noticing that her grandfather's hair wasn't wet at all.

"Well, I'm fine," Duncan said with a smile. "But I think I'm getting a cold. I'm going to take a little nap."

"Good idea," said Kelly. Then she heard a muffled thump from inside, as if something had fallen.

Duncan looked behind him and shifted his weight as though he was nervous about something.

"What was that?" Kelly asked. "Did something fall?"

"I don't know. I had some big boxes stacked up in the kitchen. Must have toppled over."

"Oh," said Kelly, growing more and more curious. "Want me to help you pick them up?"

"No, no! I'm fine. I think I'll just go take that nap now. Tell your mom I'm fine and I'll see you all a little later."

He closed the door, as though in a real hurry. Kelly stood there for a minute, trying to find a reason for her grandpa's unusual behavior. He almost always invited her in for tea when she stopped by. He always looked glad to see her!

Kelly trudged back to the warm kitchen. "He's okay," she told her mom in a small voice.

"Good!" said Laura. "Everyone is safe and sound! Let Christmas come!"

"Mom?" Kelly began. "When you saw Grandpa come home, was he alone?"

"Of course. What makes you ask?"

"I don't know." Kelly shrugged. "It sounded as

if someone was in his house, and he didn't want me to come inside."

"That's strange. I'm sure he was alone. But maybe one of his friends stopped by."

"There are no cars parked outside," Kelly commented.

"Maybe someone walked over."

"Mom, does Grandpa know people here? I mean, has he made friends in Redville?"

"Sure," said Laura. "You know how friendly he is. He's told us about some of the other antique collectors he's met around town, and I know he had dinner with two men he met at the Senior Center. Oh, and he and Perry went to a movie together last week — they both love those spy movies!"

"That's nice." Kelly smiled. "I'm glad he's making friends."

But has he told you about Celeste? she wanted to ask.

"You know," Laura said thoughtfully, "I bet it's Perry who came over. That's probably who you heard in the carriage house. I saw him out earlier shoveling snow."

"Probably," sighed Kelly. *But if it was Perry, then why didn't he invite me in, too?*

Kelly had a sneaking suspicion that Celeste was visiting the carriage house. And she couldn't wait to talk to Mia about it when they shared Christmas Eve dinner together later that evening.

"You mean Mrs. Gibson switched the dogs?" Mia exclaimed. "I can't believe it!"

Mia and Kelly and Sophie were playing in Mia's room while the grown-ups finished preparing the Christmas Eve feast. Glorious smells wafted from the kitchen, making Kelly's mouth water. Sophie jumped in and out of the girls' laps, and tumbled across the bottom bunk bed.

"Actually, her daughter got them confused," Kelly explained.

"Well, it's not hard to see why," said Mia. "They look just alike."

"I know. But I think Oscar is just a little bit bigger — especially his paws."

"Wow!" said Mia, closing her eyes. "I wonder where Oscar is! I'm trying to visualize where he might be."

"Any luck?" Kelly asked after a few minutes.

"Not really," Mia admitted. "I hope he's happy, though."

"Me too," said Kelly. "Oh, Mia — guess what?"

"What?" asked Mia, reaching over to cuddle Sophie.

"Don't say a word, but I think Celeste was visiting my grandpa today at the carriage house."

"You're kidding!" whispered Mia. "So, the romance really is happening. It's just like what happened with my grandma! Do you think they'll get married?"

"I don't know. But Mia — the thing that's worrying me is the part about her being allergic to dogs!"

"I forgot that part! Well, if they get married,

then you would get to keep Sophie. I mean Oscar. This is too confusing."

"You're telling me!" said Kelly. "I've had a stomachache all day. I can't wait until tomorrow morning when the surprise will finally be over!"

Kelly suddenly realized that with all her attention focused on Oscar these past weeks, she'd had little time to think about the excitement of Christmas morning. She had hardly thought about presents or stockings — or about the wonderful dinner she was going to enjoy with her best friend and their families. Even with all the dog craziness, there was still so much to look forward to. She couldn't wait to give Mia her gift — a copy of the big book of dog breeds they'd first looked at in the university library. And she hoped her mom would like the special ornament painted by Joni and that her dad would appreciate a new blue sweater.

"Hey," said Mia, "where is your grandpa, anyway?"

"That's the weird part," sighed Kelly. "He says he has a cold and doesn't feel well. He said he didn't want to pass his cold on to anyone else, so he thought he'd stay home and rest."

"But I already have a cold," Mia said. Then she coughed a couple of times for good measure.

"I know — we told him. But he can be very stubborn sometimes."

"We were all hoping he would come," said Mia. "Perry even rented a couple of spy movies for later."

"Do you think —?" Kelly began and then stopped.

"What?"

"Do you think he's spending Christmas Eve with Celeste and that's why he's not coming over?"

"I doubt it," said Mia hopefully. "Remember, she has a grandson. Wouldn't she want to be with him?"

"You're right," said Kelly. "And when Mom came back from taking some food over to the carriage house, she said Grandpa sounded like he had a really stuffy nose."

"So everything's fine!" Mia concluded. "Isn't it, Sophie?"

Sophie put her front paws on Mia's chest and gave her a wet lick in response. Then Bo and Chubby scratched at the bedroom door until Mia let them in, holding Sophie against her chest.

"They're so jealous," Mia observed. "Look at them — they can't stand it that I'm holding a puppy."

The two dogs sniffed at Sophie and then wandered over to Kelly for some attention. "It's okay," she offered. "I still love you both. You were the first dogs in my life." She petted and soothed them until they curled up next to her, ignoring Sophie completely.

The dining room table was set with china and candles and some of the Christmas ornaments made by Mia's mom. Everything looked beautiful and elegant, Kelly thought. Like something out of a magazine. Joni and David always made Christmas Eve at their house a wonderful occasion.

Kelly took her place between Mia and Perry and looked at all the happy faces around her. Everyone was smiling and laughing, admiring the decorations and the delicious smells from the kitchen. The only thing missing was Grandpa Dunc.

This feels like Christmas! thought Kelly. *My family, our good friends, three dogs, good food, and a warm house safe from the blizzard outside!*

As they did each year, everyone at the table took turns making a toast. Glasses were raised to good health, to good friends, and to success in the coming year. Perry toasted good grades in the coming semester and Ben toasted good gigs for his band. Mia toasted all the dogs in the world, especially Sophie and Oscar — wherever he was!

When it was Kelly's turn, she felt a small wave of emotion wash over her. She raised her glass of sparkling cider and said, "I would like to drink a toast to Grandpa Dunc and his first Christmas living with us — and I wish he were here at the table."

"Here, here!" said half the table.

"To Grandpa Dunc!" said the other half.

Laura reached across the table and took Kelly's hand in hers. "That was lovely," she said. "Merry Christmas!"

"Merry Christmas," Kelly answered. Then she peered under the table where Sophie was sleeping. "Merry Christmas, little Westie!"

TEN

The Westie Christmas Morning

Kelly was awake before anyone else in the household — except for Sophie, who pranced around the bedroom, eager to begin the day.

"Hey," said Kelly, reaching down to rub Sophie's ears, "Merry Christmas! Today's the day we present you to Grandpa Dunc!"

Sophie wiggled in response, wanting nothing more than to hop up on Kelly's bed and snuggle. Already Kelly felt very attached to Sophie. She was amazed at how much she had bonded with the puppy in less than twenty-four hours.

"You know what?" said Kelly, bringing Sophie up on the bed. "It's going to be hard to give you back. But . . . someone is missing you right now. Someone is wishing you were waiting underneath their tree. And you missed your litter mates last night, didn't you? You whined quite a bit! But I didn't mind."

Sophie barked in response, and Kelly was glad that Grandpa Dunc lived in the carriage house. It wasn't easy to keep an excited, vocal puppy a secret for very long. Kelly sat up and stretched, wondering what time it was. It was still mostly dark, so she knew it was very early. She looked out her bedroom window to see if the snow had let up.

The backyard was absolutely beautiful! Kelly watched as the sun rose slowly, painting stripes of pale pink and yellow to the east. It had stopped snowing, but the ground and trees were covered with dense, sparkly snow.

What a perfect Christmas morning! Kelly thought, holding Sophie close.

And then she noticed that the carriage house was filled with light. It was nice to know that Grandpa was up early, too. She hoped he was looking forward to Christmas morning as much as she was. She bit her bottom lip, wishing with all her heart that her surprise would make Duncan happy.

Carrying Sophie, Kelly marched into her parents' room. As she had expected, they were still asleep. Kelly decided that a wet kiss from Sophie would be the perfect alarm clock. She released the dog, who bounced happily between the sleeping bodies, looking for a face to lick.

"What?" John murmured as Sophie found his forehead. "Hmm?"

Next, Laura received several licks on her ear. She sat up quickly, then laughed when she discovered Sophie sitting next to her, an expectant look in her black eyes.

"Well, good morning, Miss Sophie," Laura said. "Don't tell me — Kelly sent you to get us out of bed."

"Well," Kelly said, "it *is* Christmas morning. And Grandpa's already up — I saw his lights on."

"You're all crazy," John mumbled. "It's the middle of the night!"

"Sorry," said Laura, "but it's actually seven A.M. I'll start the coffee."

"Mom?" said Kelly. "How exactly should I give Grandpa the dog?"

Laura thought this over, petting Sophie as she sorted through the possibilities. "I think," she announced finally, "that you'd better do it right away. If you don't, I'm afraid Sophie will bark and spoil the surprise."

"I'm going to call him and tell him to hurry over right now! I can't wait any longer!"

When Kelly heard the back door open, she ran to meet Grandpa Dunc. "Merry Christmas!" she shouted, hugging him hard. "I can't wait to give you your present!"

"Whoa!" said Duncan, holding on to the door frame so he wouldn't fall over. "Merry Christmas yourself! You're pretty excited this morning, aren't you?"

"I've been waiting and waiting to give you your present and today is the day!"

"Well," said Laura, coming into the kitchen, "go ahead."

"Wait!" John said. "Let me get the camera. I have to take advantage of this photo opportunity."

"This must be some present," said Duncan. "Shouldn't we have breakfast first?"

"We can't!" Kelly laughed, jumping up and down. "Come with me!"

She led Duncan into the living room and sat him down in the chair closest to the Christmas tree. "You have to wait here for just a minute," she directed. "And you have to close your eyes!"

Duncan put his hands over his eyes, shaking his head in wonder. Laura stood in the doorway watching, and John knelt down, checking angles for his camera.

"Ready?" Kelly whispered to Sophie, carrying her down the stairs. "Now, you have to be quiet. No barking allowed!"

For some reason, Sophie cooperated and nestled quietly in Kelly's arms. Kelly tiptoed up to her grandpa. "Keep your eyes closed and hold out your hands." He did as he was instructed, and Kelly leaned forward and placed the little Westie in his outstretched arms.

Duncan's eyes flew open. He made a small gasping sound and stared at the puppy in his arms. The color seemed to drain from his face. John snapped a few pictures. Sophie raised her chin to sniff the new person who was holding her. Duncan stared and stared, not saying a word.

Kelly asked hesitantly, "Grandpa? Are you all right? Is it — do you — did I —?"

Duncan looked at Kelly and then at Sophie. "Where did you get this dog?"

"From a breeder. But Grandpa — it's not the dog you were supposed to get! You were supposed to get her brother, but — oh, I have such a long story to tell you."

Duncan looked so strange and unhappy that Kelly ran to her mother and hid her face in Laura's robe. *I made a mistake!* she thought. *Everyone was right — my surprise backfired! Grandpa isn't happy at all!*

John stopped taking photos and Laura hugged her daughter close. "It's okay, honey," she told Kelly. "Don't cry, honey."

Duncan set Sophie on the floor and went quickly over to Kelly. "Don't cry," he repeated. "Kelly, please stop crying. I have someone I want you to meet. But you have to promise to stop crying. Sit down and wait just a minute. I'm going to go get my friend and I'll be right back."

Duncan disappeared with an air of mystery. Sophie ran over to Kelly and nuzzled her slippers, trying to give some comfort to her sad human friend. But Kelly couldn't stop crying.

"He's going to get Celeste!" Kelly blurted out between sobs. "Grandpa hates the dog and he's going to get Celeste and she's allergic to dogs!"

"What?" asked John.

"What are you talking about?" said Laura. "Do you mean Celeste from the holiday show?"

But before Kelly could explain about Cuts Are Us and ring boxes, Duncan reappeared carrying a huge green box. And he was alone! Just Duncan and the enormous box.

"Your turn to open a gift," Duncan announced. "And you'd better hurry!"

Kelly wiped her eyes and approached the big box. There were a million questions she wanted to ask her grandpa, but instead she lifted the lid of the box and peered inside.

"Oh!" she cried. "Oh, no! I don't believe it! *I don't believe it!*"

"What?" said John and Laura, hurrying over.

Kelly reached inside and pulled out a Westie puppy identical to Sophie.

"I don't believe it!" said Kelly's parents in unison.

"And I don't believe it, either!" Duncan laughed, wiping a tear from his eye. "If this isn't the craziest Christmas on record, I'll run around the block barefoot!"

"Who?" asked Kelly, her mouth hanging open. "How? When?" She couldn't even form the right words to ask the right questions.

Then suddenly the room was in an uproar as the puppy wriggled out of Kelly's arms and ran to play with Sophie. The two dogs chased around the room, biting playfully at each other's necks and growling happily.

"Well," sighed Duncan, "I think what we have here is a brother-sister Christmas reunion."

"You mean," said Kelly, suddenly understanding, "you mean the dog you just gave me is *Oscar*?"

"Yep," said Duncan. "And the dog you gave me has to be Sophie!"

Kelly was so stunned she couldn't talk. She just watched as the two dogs took turns jumping on each other and running between all available furniture legs and human legs. For a few minutes, no one spoke. Everyone watched the two dogs, trying to take in the strange coincidence of double Westie Christmas gifts.

"How long have you been planning to give Kelly a dog?" John finally asked. He'd put his camera down, unable to stand the suspense. And his subjects were moving too fast to photograph, anyway.

"Ever since I moved here. I thought being an only child, Kelly would enjoy having a dog as a companion. And I could see how much she loved them from the way she acted around Bo and Chubby."

"And I wanted to get *you* a dog so you wouldn't be lonely when we were all away," Kelly put in. "And so that you'd feel more at home."

"But how did you pick a Westie?" Laura asked Duncan. "We know how Kelly chose one — because she saw how much you liked the one at the animal shelter."

"But that's why I chose a Westie, too," Duncan said with a laugh. "That day at the shelter, I saw Kelly and Mia linger forever at the kennel, falling in love with that little white dog."

"Only it was already adopted!" Kelly exclaimed.

"Right," said Duncan. "So this friend of mine, a woman who cuts my hair —"

Uh-oh, here it comes! thought Kelly.

"— she told me about a breeder she knew out in the country."

"Mrs. Gibson!" said Kelly.

"Right. So I went to see her, and arranged to buy Sophie for you for Christmas."

"And the animal shelter volunteer told *me* about Mrs. Gibson, and I arranged to buy Oscar for *you*!"

"And the rest is history," sighed John.

"It's interesting," said Laura. "Mathematically speaking, there is little statistical possibility that two people in the same family would unknowingly buy two dogs from the same breeder, and then bring home opposite dogs because of a random human error. It's fascinating!"

"All I know," said Duncan, "is that one and one equals two, and we now have two dogs! What are we going to do?"

"Do you like your surprise, Grandpa?" Kelly asked. "Aside from what's happened?"

"Oh, Kelly, it's the best Christmas present anyone ever gave me. And I know from my own experience how difficult it must have been for you to make all the arrangements, try to cover your tracks, and keep the surprise a surprise."

"You can say that again!" said Kelly, flopping to the floor in a display of exhaustion.

"Is that why you didn't come to Christmas Eve dinner?" Laura asked.

"Well, I didn't want to leave the little guy alone. He seemed pretty scared."

"I took Sophie to Mia's," said Kelly, "when I found out you weren't coming."

"And how about that time I saw you outside the pet store," Duncan recalled. "You were on your way out, and I was on my way in to buy a dog collar."

"That was a close call!" Kelly laughed. "That was the same day I saw you —" She stopped mid-sentence, clamping her jaw shut tight.

"What?" asked John. "Saw him what?"

"I thought," Kelly tried to explain, "we thought — Mia and Perry and I — that Grandpa was — that he had a —"

"Had a what?" Duncan asked with curiosity.

"A girlfriend," Kelly squeaked in a tiny voice. Everyone in the room stared at her.

"A girlfriend?" Duncan repeated, sounding very amused by the idea. "What in the world gave you that notion?"

Knowing there was no way out, Kelly tried to explain. "We saw you go to Cuts Are Us after the pet shop. You were — you were laughing with Celeste and then you gave her the ring box."

"A ring?" Laura gasped. "Dad?"

Duncan laughed hard now, slapping his knee and gulping for air. Kelly had never seen him laugh like that. "Kelly," he said, when he finally contained himself, "Celeste is my friend. Just a friend. We laugh together all the time when she cuts my hair. She's a funny lady."

"But what about the ring?" Kelly asked. She wasn't sure if she felt relieved or disappointed that

Celeste and Duncan were only friends. It had been sort of fun, she realized now, to think of them having a secret romance.

"It wasn't a ring," Duncan explained. "I gave her a gift for helping me locate a dog for you. It was an antique key ring I found on one of my treasure hunts. It was just a little thank-you present."

"I thought you were — Mia and I thought you were, you know —" Kelly was too embarrassed to finish.

"You'd be one of the first people to know, I promise," Duncan said softly. "If I ever have the good fortune to find someone half as wonderful as your grandma, I would tell my family straight away. It wouldn't be a secret."

"But what about Celeste?" asked Kelly shyly. "She seems awfully nice."

"She is nice. But we barely know each other."

"And don't forget," Kelly reminded him, "she's allergic to dogs. That had me really worried when I thought you two were — you know . . ."

"Well," said Duncan thoughtfully, "didn't Mrs.

Gibson tell you that Westies don't shed? And that they are almost completely free of odor?"

This made everyone laugh. And the laughter made Oscar and Sophie stop their running and re- gard the circle of humans around the Christmas tree.

"I wonder what they're thinking?" Kelly said.

"I think they're pretty happy to be together," Laura observed. "Just look at them."

"Are we going to keep them both?" Kelly asked hopefully.

"Well," said Duncan, "it wouldn't seem fair to split them up again, now would it?"

"But who will take care of them?" asked John. "I hate to sound like a party pooper but —"

"I will!" declared Duncan. "All my life I had at least two dogs. Sometimes on the farm we had a good deal more than that. And I have a feeling Kelly will be more than willing to help me when she's home from school."

"Oh, I will!" cried Kelly. She leaned over and

hugged Duncan tight. "Thank you, Grandpa! This is the best Christmas ever!"

"It's going to be a winter of Westies," Duncan said, laughing. "Hold on to your hats!"

"Hey, Grandpa!" said Kelly. "How about if we get dressed and take these guys out in the snow for a few minutes. We have leashes and collars!"

"It's a deal. How about it, doggies? Are you ready for the Westie winter to begin?"

Oscar and Sophie ran to Duncan, licking his outstretched hand. The two small white dogs nuzzling her grandfather was one of the most delightful scenes Kelly had ever had the pleasure of witnessing.

"The Westie winter!" sighed Kelly happily. "Let the fun begin!"

Facts About
West Highland Terriers

1. The West Highland White Terrier was recognized as a breed by the British Kennel Club in 1907.
2. The Westie is small, but strongly built, weighing about 15 to 22 pounds and growing to a height of 11 inches. They are always pure white, with a wiry, flat topcoat, and a soft, close undercoat. They have a black nose, dark eyes, black nails and footpads, with straight, jaunty tails.
3. The Westie is courageous and agile and has great stamina.
4. Westies originated in Scotland and were first

bred by Colonel Edward Donald Malcolm.

5. They are closely related to the scottie, cairn, Dandie Dinmont, and other rough-haired terriers of Scotland.

6. Westies were originally bred to hunt fox and otter on Scottish farms.

7. Westies do not shed and are virtually odor-free.

8. Westies are sweet, loyal, and loving, but they have great self-esteem. They are intelligent, feisty, and rarely subservient!

These facts were compiled from two books:

Faherty, Ruth. *Westies From Head to Tail*. Loveland, CO: Alpine Blue Ribbon Books, 1989.

The Reader's Digest Illustrated Book of Dogs, rev. 2nd ed. Pleasantville, NY: The Reader's Digest Association, Inc., 1983.

About the Author

Growing up in Denver, Colorado, Coleen Hubbard liked to write and put on plays in her backyard. As an adult, she still writes plays. She also now writes for children and young adults. Among her works are four books in the Treasured Horses series, which sparked her interest in writing fun books about animals and kids.

Coleen and her husband have three dog-crazy young daughters, plus Maggie the Magnificent, a sweet-natured mixed breed who inspired Coleen to learn all about the various breeds of dogs featured in the Dog Tales series.